80 002 275 545

Northamptonshire County Council
Libraries and I...

06 FEB 04
14. FEB 04
06 MAR 04
1/5/04
22. JUN 04
27. JUL 04

14/1x/05

Northamptonshire
Book Sales
PAID

GORDON, A.

Saving Suzannah

BH 5-01	1/04			

Please return or renew this item by the last date shown.
You may renew items (unless they have been requested
by another customer) by telephoning, writing to or calling
in at any library.   100% recycled paper   BKS 1 (5/95)

Abigail Gordon is fascinated by words, and what better way to use them than in the crafting of romance between the sexes? A state of the heart that has affected almost everyone at some time of their lives. Twice widowed, she now lives alone in a Cheshire village. Her two eldest sons between themselves have presented her with three delightful grandchildren, and her youngest son lives nearby.

Recent titles by the same author:

THE ELUSIVE DOCTOR
FINGER ON THE PULSE
SAVING FACES

SAVING SUZANNAH

BY
ABIGAIL GORDON

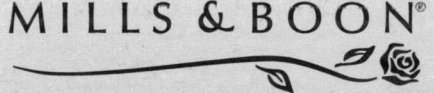

For Jackie, who brought me to Grenfell's land

DID YOU PURCHASE THIS BOOK WITHOUT A COVER?

If you did, you should be aware it is **stolen property** as it was reported *unsold and destroyed* by a retailer. Neither the author nor the publisher has received any payment for this book.

All the characters in this book have no existence outside the imagination of the author, and have no relation whatsoever to anyone bearing the same name or names. They are not even distantly inspired by any individual known or unknown to the author, and all the incidents are pure invention.

All Rights... part in... Harlequ... thereof... means, e... storage...

This boo... trade or... without... cover ot... condition...

MILLS & BOON and MILLS & BOON with the Rose Device are registered trademarks of the publisher.

First published in Great Britain 2001
Harlequin Mills & Boon Limited,
Eton House, 18-24 Paradise Road, Richmond, Surrey TW9 1SR

© Abigail Gordon 2001

ISBN 0 263 82666 X

Set in Times Roman 10½ on 11½ pt.
03-0501-52433

Printed and bound in Spain
by Litografia Rosés, S.A., Barcelona

NORTHAMPTONSHIRE LIBRARIES	
80002275545	
H J	24/04/2001
F	£2.49

CHAPTER ONE

GOLDEN fronds of fern moved gently in the breeze beside the grey, wind-stripped bark of the trees as Suzannah climbed the steep path through the woods.

Newfoundland in the fall was a pleasant surprise, she thought as the September sun danced amongst the changing leaves. It was incredible to think that in just a matter of weeks this rugged land of lakes, rivers and the endlessly embracing sea would be in the grip of a winter that would make England's cold months seem merely chilly. But if what John and Debbie had told her was correct, that was how it would be.

Yet today was like an autumn day at home and she was here to do something that she'd been promising herself ever since arriving.

There had been plenty of opportunities to accomplish it before these last days when winter was hovering, but she'd held back, knowing that an outing such as today's might open a wound that was only partly healed.

Suzannah had arrived in St Anthony in the spring when icebergs could be seen out at sea. Broken away from the glaciers and magnificent in freedom, they'd looked like huge sculptures of pale blue frosted glass floating past.

'They're the most beautiful things I've ever seen,' she'd exclaimed.

Her youthful hosts had smiled. 'They can be dangerous, too, don't forget,' her brother John had said wryly. 'Remember the *Titanic*? It wasn't that far away from here where it went down.'

'It doesn't make me any less entranced,' she'd insisted.

'I'd want to live here for ever if I could see that sight from my window every day.'

'They'll soon be gone,' his wife Debbie had told her. 'As the weather gets warmer they start to break up, but we'll be sighting them for a few more weeks yet.'

However, the weather and its caprices were the last thing on her mind today. She was about to delve into the past. Her pilgrimage up the hillside was something she'd known she was going to do from the moment she'd set foot on the island.

It was one reason why she'd accepted the invitation for an extended stay with John and his family in St Anthony. There was another motive behind it, too, with deeper, painful connotations, but she was determined that it wasn't going to eat at her today.

Suzannah had come to pay tribute to a man from her home town in England, who had captured her imagination years ago, and as the path suddenly widened into a clearing high on the hillside she knew that the moment was upon her.

The words on a bronze plaque fastened to a rockface in front of her were what she'd come to read, and as her eyes fastened on the inscription she experienced the strangest feeling.

As if the path of her life, which had been proving to be as steep a climb as the one she'd just done up Tea House Hill, was about to level out like this clearing where his ashes were buried.

WILFRED THOMASON GRENFELL, it said on the plaque. BORN FEBRUARY 28TH 1865—DIED OCTOBER 9TH 1940, and underneath, so applicable that it brought a lump to her throat, LIFE IS A FIELD OF HONOUR.

Suzannah felt tears prick. It was this man, the fearless healer of the sick and poor amongst the fishing communities of Newfoundland and the Inuits of Labrador, who had inspired her to take up medicine.

And what had she done? she asked herself despairingly. Allowed a distressing incident to blight her career!

In her formative years she'd been fascinated by the story of Wilfred Grenfell, the doctor from the ancient city of Chester where she lived.

A man of high ideals, born to serve his fellow men, he had gone as agent of the National Mission to Deep Sea Fishermen in 1892 to the remote island of Newfoundland, intent on establishing a system of health care for the fishermen whose livelihood had kept them apart from the larger communities on Newfoundland.

But being the man he was, Grenfell had ended up doing much more than that. For the first time ever he'd brought medical care to the Inuits living across the Belle Isle straits in Labrador, an even more inaccessible place than Newfoundland.

In later years he'd founded the Grenfell Mission in St Anthony, a centre for medical care and philanthropy and the first of its kind in that part of the world.

Now renamed the Charles S. Curtis Memorial Hospital, after one of the doctors he'd persuaded to work with him all those years ago, the huge hospital building stood at the bottom of the hill that she'd just climbed.

The sheer single-mindedness of Grenfell's dedication to the humble fisherfolk of the two islands, where the moose population equalled one to every five humans, had fired Suzannah's youthful imagination.

All right. She hadn't made it to the frozen north like he had. She'd worked in a hospital in the Midlands and had loved her job, until the incident had occurred which had all but ruined her life.

Since then she'd been living in St Anthony in self-imposed exile with John, his Canadian wife Debbie and their two young sons, Robbie and Richard.

'Impressive, wasn't he?' a voice said from on high in the quiet clearing, and Suzannah swung round, startled. She'd thought she'd had the place where Grenfell's ashes were buried to herself, but she'd been wrong.

A man was standing on a raised wooden platform in a secluded corner of the clearing, and as she observed him with surprised hazel eyes he came slowly down the steps.

For a moment she thought he might be a gardener. There had been one or two working in the grounds as she'd made her way up the hill path, but though his clothes were casual enough they weren't the attire one would have expected of a manual worker.

As the rest of him came into view Suzannah caught her breath. Beneath hair of honey gold, eyes of the same deep blue as the mighty Atlantic were observing her with frank approval. He was big and wholesome-looking, so much so that she couldn't believe that she'd missed seeing him there.

She could only think that her absorption in the legend whose name was spoken with reverence wherever one went in Newfoundland must have blinded her to the presence of the most attractive man she'd ever seen.

'Yes, he *was* impressive...very,' she said, finding her voice at last.

'Ah! You're English,' he commented. 'Come to pay homage to a countryman?'

Suzannah smiled for the first time since setting foot on Tea House Hill. 'Yes, that's right. Grenfell came from the same place as myself.'

'Chester?'

Her eyes widened. 'Yes. How did you know?'

The man smiled, showing strong white teeth. 'There's not much I don't know about him. My great-grandfather was one of the first to be treated by him. He had frostbite in his leg, which wasn't an uncommon thing in those days. And if Grenfell hadn't got to him in time he would have had to hack it off himself and take his chances. But, like the messenger of God that he was, the doc came sledging through the snow with his dog team and—'

'Saved the leg?'

His smile widened. 'No. He amputated it, but in the proper manner, and where my ancestor would have risked all sorts of infections if he'd done it himself, within weeks he was mobile on something unheard of in those parts—a prosthesis, which, in case you don't know, is an artificial leg.'

'I do know what a prosthesis is,' Suzannah said quietly. 'I'm a doctor myself.'

The stranger threw back his head and laughed. 'I don't believe it. If any more turn up we'll have enough for a convention.'

'I'm not with you,' she said slowly.

'You, myself...and Grenfell, although his would have to be a non-participating role, I'm afraid.'

'You're in the medical profession, too?'

'Lafe Hilliard at your service, ma'am. General surgeon and jack of all trades. Late of a far colder place than this and now back in my home town of St Anthony.'

'I haven't seen you around,' Suzannah said without thinking, and immediately wished she hadn't. It was as good as saying that she would have remembered if she had.

'You wouldn't have,' he informed her. 'I only arrived back home yesterday.' With friendly inquisitiveness he added, 'And what about you, English doctor? What is your name...and what are you doing in St Anthony?'

She hesitated. She'd been interested enough to question the blond Viking about his affairs, but did she want to tell him hers?

He was waiting, his bright blue gaze taking in every detail of her fine-boned slenderness and the smooth chestnut hair swept back from a face that was beautiful, though at the same time the mirror of a mind that lacked tranquillity.

Her eyes were its most striking feature, clear hazel pools, but there was unhappiness in them, and although her mouth had the warm curves of generosity it drooped.

'My name is Suzannah Scott,' she said, breaking the silence. 'I'm on an extended visit to my brother and his family here in St Anthony.'

'And because he came from the place where you live, you're here to see where Grenfell's ashes lie?'

Suzannah nodded. 'And you? Why are you here?'

'Obviously it's something we have in common. Our respect for a great man. I always come to this place when I'm home. Have you seen inside his house?'

Suzannah shook her head. 'No. That is my next port of call. I passed it on the way up.'

'Maybe we could view it together.' She eyed him doubtfully. 'After all, we do have the common bond.'

'But surely you've seen it before...if you live in St Anthony?'

'Dozens of times, but not in the company of an English doctor.'

'Lead on, then, Lafe Hilliard,' she said, entering into the spirit of the thing with this friendly stranger. 'Show me Grenfell's house.'

The home of the intrepid doctor was a museum now, with polished wooden floors that shone like mirrors and a rug made from the skin of a polar bear lying in creamy magnificence in front of the fireplace in the sitting room. The walls were painted in warm rose red and soft green, with heavy furniture from a past age standing against them.

Suzannah could imagine Grenfell coming back to this

haven after sledging across the ice with his dogs to attend the sick of Newfoundland. Or coming home after crossing the straits from Labrador where he'd been treating the Inuits for whom he'd had such respect.

As they went from room to room she was aware of the sea on all sides. The harbour wasn't far away. It was that seascape that Lafe Hilliard had been absorbed in when she'd arrived in the clearing at the top of the hill, and it could still be seen from where they were now.

'It's lovely,' she breathed when they ended up back in the sitting room again after touring the rest of the house. 'It's old but very gracious. I'd like to live in it myself.'

'Me, too,' he said, and added with a smile, 'With one or two innovations maybe.'

She'd left the hire car that she was using on the hospital forecourt, and as they walked back towards it a moment of awkwardness descended.

They were strangers. An hour ago they hadn't known each other. Yet she'd felt more relaxed in this man's presence than she'd been in months.

However, it was time to say goodbye. It wasn't in her nature to presume upon casual acquaintance and yet the right words to end this pleasant time with him wouldn't come to her tongue.

Instead, she said, 'Being the doctor that you are, and living in St Anthony as you do, I would have expected you to be based here at the Curtis Memorial Hospital.'

He shook his head. 'No. 'Fraid not. I'm a fellow who never takes the easy way out.'

Suzannah nodded. That was something else they had in common. She could have taken the easy way out back in England and convinced herself there was nothing to feel guilty about, but she hadn't and the future looked bleaker than a Canadian winter.

Lafe Hilliard was changing the subject. 'I think that after

climbing the hill and doing the rounds of Wilfred's place we owe ourselves a coffee. What do you think?'

'I think that's a good idea,' she replied with a lifting of spirit, 'but…'

His sigh was heart-rending, yet it only made her laugh.

'How did I know there was going to be a but?'

'I was about to say that I can't be long. My sister-in-law is away at the moment. She and my brother both work for the Bank of Montreal and Debbie is in Corner Brook, doing some promotional work, which means that I pick the children up from school.'

'Right, then let's move,' he said, and pointing to the nearby shopping mall, 'That's the nearest place.'

'And so you have your brother and his family close by. Are there any other important people in your life, Suzannah?' he asked when they were seated inside a small coffee-shop in the mall.

She hesitated. Did she want to tell this golden-haired son of Newfoundland that, apart from her brother and his family, there was no one? It was a pitiful admission to have to make, but at that moment it was true.

It hadn't been the case six months ago. She'd been quietly happy, doing the job she'd always wanted to do and at the same time looking forward to marrying the hospital's top surgeon.

It had been the arrogance and ambition that had driven Nigel Summers towards the top that could have been his downfall, but Suzannah had been the one who'd taken on the burden of guilt.

Lafe knew he was being nosy and wasn't sure why. Maybe it was because she was English. There was a certain style about her and she was very beautiful in a restrained sort of way, but he sensed sadness in her. He could feel it, and he wondered what had happened to damp her down, because damped down she was.

'There's no one,' Suzannah said with reluctant honesty. 'Except for John, Debbie and the boys.'

With her head bent, she didn't see his eyes brighten as she went on to say, 'I've come to stay in Newfoundland for an indefinite period. As far as my brother and his wife are concerned, I could stay for ever...and I might just do that.'

'So you're not committed to any hospital back home, then?'

The question was innocent enough. He had no idea that he'd just turned a blade in her heart.

'No, I'm not committed to anyone or anywhere,' she said quietly, and knew that if he asked any more questions she would have to tell him to mind his own business. Not because she minded him asking, but because the answers were so painful to make.

But for some reason he must have sensed that he was treading on forbidden ground, and with the easy camaraderie that was casting its spell over her he started to talk about general things.

In no time at all she had to tell him that she was going to have to go and pick up her nephews, and with an understanding nod he got to his feet.

'Where do your relatives live?' he asked as she stood, poised for flight.

It was a casual enough question, but Suzannah knew that the answer to it would either turn their acquaintance into a continuing thing or finish it here and now.

She didn't want it to finish but neither did she want any more heartache, and at the present time that was what relationships meant.

So she waved a vague hand towards the harbour front and said, 'Over on the far side of town.' And waited to see if he pursued it.

He didn't. Lafe merely nodded and held out a large, capable hand for her to shake. 'Nice to have met you, Suzannah Scott. Enjoy your stay in my beautiful country.'

'I'll try,' she told him with regret inside her now that she'd put the blight on any further communication between them.

'Goodbye, Lafe,' she said, and because of that same regret she went on, 'I shall remember our meeting.'

'Good. And whatever it is that's hurting, don't let it. Life is too short, Suzannah.' With an easy, loping stride he moved off in the direction of the hospital grounds once more.

As she drove to the school Suzannah couldn't stop thinking about him. Why had he gone towards the hospital when he wasn't employed there? she wondered. And he hadn't arrived by car from wherever he'd come from.

Lafe had been curious enough about her affairs, but he hadn't been forthcoming with any details of his own life, except for the information that he was a doctor, and that had been mainly a bald statement of fact.

'So what?' she said to no one in particular. Did it matter? They were unlikely to ever meet again, so perhaps it was as well that they hadn't exchanged too many confidences.

John, Debbie and the children had been her life-savers during the long empty summer. Her brother and his wife had been there for her when she'd needed them and had left her alone when she'd wanted time to herself.

At ten and seven years old respectively, Richard and Robbie loved having her as part of the household, and their affection had been like a balm to her aching heart.

As they came spilling out of school it was the same as always—Robbie hurtling towards her with tie askew, schoolbag overflowing, and Richard, with a youthful gravity that Suzannah found totally endearing, following on at a slower pace.

With their mother away in Corner Brook, she was in

charge of the evening meal, and when John came in the four of them ate together.

As they took their seats at the table he asked, 'And what sort of a day have you had, sis?'

They were alike in appearance—hazel eyes, brown hair and of a similar build—but quite different when it came to personality.

Her brother was a confident, no-nonsense type. He'd urged her frequently to assert herself with the hospital board back home, which she might have done if the hurt hadn't been inflicted by the man she'd been engaged to, making what had happened twice as painful.

Suzannah smiled. 'It's been great.'

John eyed her in surprise. It was the first time she'd shown that sort of enthusiasm.

'Really? So what have you been up to?'

'I went to see where Wilfred Grenfell's ashes are buried on the hill above the harbour.'

'Ah, of course. Your hero, isn't he?'

She nodded, 'And then I was taken on a tour of his house.'

'Yes, they do guided tours around the place. I can remember Debbie and I being shown round when we first came to live in St Anthony.'

'This was spontaneous.'

John looked up from his plate and Richard asked, 'What does "spontaneous" mean, 'Zannah?'

'It means that it wasn't planned,' she told him. 'It was something I did on the spur of the moment…er…with someone I'd met up on the hillside.'

'Do you mean a stranger?' her brother asked, almost choking on his food and then answering his own question. 'It would have to be as you don't know anyone here, apart from ourselves.'

'I do now,' she said, and was surprised at the pleasure it gave her to say so.

'His name is Lafe Hilliard. He's just arrived back in St Anthony from somewhere or other, and guess what, Johnnie?'

'What?'

'He's one of us.'

The two boys had been listening, round-eyed, and now Robbie asked, 'You mean he's one of our family, 'Zannah?'

'No, darling,' she said gently. 'I meant that he's a doctor, like me.'

'I don't have to be told who and what Lafe Hilliard is,' her brother said with the surprise still upon him. 'He's the son of one of the oldest families in St Anthony and has recently become the last of the line.'

'You mean that all his relatives are dead?'

'Yes.'

'And he hasn't got children of his own to carry on the name?'

'No. Not officially anyway. It was in the local paper the other day that he was due back, and from what you say he's obviously arrived.'

'Where has he come back from?' she asked. 'He didn't go into details.'

'The guy has spent the last two years in the Arctic on one of the stations doing research into global warming. He was resident medical officer there but came back because his father died. I guess he's got a lot of loose ends to tie up.'

It was Suzannah's turn to goggle. No wonder he'd been relishing the mellow autumn day. He'd been living where the only thing to be seen had been snow and more snow. A doctor on ice. Yet there'd been nothing cold about him. In fact, meeting him had taken the chill out of her heart for the first time since she'd left England. But that was going to be the extent of it.

Nigel Summers had put the blight on any future liaisons with the opposite sex, and if she lived to be a hundred she wasn't ever going to change her mind about that.

When the boys were asleep Suzannah left John in his study and went up to her room. Inevitably she was drawn towards the window as she had been for the last few nights.

The temperature had dropped and it was a cold, clear night, the right kind of atmosphere for one of the most beautiful natural displays she'd ever seen.

As on two previous nights, there was a bright arch of green light in the sky, poised over the hills beyond the harbour. Around and beneath it were flashing arcs and countless shimmering rays which at first sight had the same green glow as the arch, but as one looked the colours changed to red, white, yellow and blinding blues.

The aurora borealis—often referred to as the northern lights—was only visible on this kind of night, in this kind of place, and it was awesome.

Brought about by electrical interactions between the earth's magnetic field and streams of energetically charged particles from the sun, it was a never-to-be-forgotten sight.

That was the basis of it, but only its splendour registered as Suzannah watched and wished, for a brief second, that there was someone to share the moment with.

Debbie arrived home from Corner Brook in the late evening of Friday, and on the Saturday Suzannah went into the town for the day so that the family could have some time to themselves.

As she wandered aimlessly around the shopping malls she was envious of the small, close-knit unit that she'd left behind, and conscious that she was drifting from one day to the next with no goal in sight.

Yet wasn't that how she'd wanted it when she'd arrived in Newfoundland in the spring? No commitments of any kind meant no quicksands to flounder in.

But the voice of reason said that it couldn't go on for ever. That she was using Nigel's betrayal as an excuse to opt out of living. Taking the coward's way out. Although there'd been nothing cowardly in the way she'd coped with being blamed for someone else's mistake.

She was standing by the cosmetics counter in one of the stores when Lafe saw her, and he smiled. When they'd separated the other day he'd told himself whimsically that if they were meant to see each other again the fates would do something about it and, lo and behold, they had!

He'd been going through his father's papers all morning and was now on his way to the solicitor's. It was decision time and he wished it wasn't.

But for the moment he was willing to be sidetracked by the sight of the chestnut-haired English doctor, the woman who'd been interested enough in her fellow countryman to walk up a steep hillside to pay her respects.

And with the thought of their own functions in health care, in an age so different to when Grenfell had practised, Lafe was curious to know why she was idling her time away here in his homeland for months on end when she could be pursuing her career.

In a lesser way he supposed that the same applied to himself. But in his case he'd flown back from Ice Station Mercury because of his father's sudden death.

There was the house, not far away from that of Grenfell's, that he had to make a decision on—whether to keep it or put it up for sale—and the old man's estate to sort out. His visit to the family solicitor this morning was the first step in that direction.

'Hello, there,' a voice said from behind as Suzannah studied the special offers on top brands of cosmetics. She recognised it immediately, and as she swung round to face him the pleasure she felt at the sound of it amazed her.

'Hello, yourself,' she said, noting that today the blond Viking was wearing a smart suit with an equally elegant shirt and tie.

'All alone?' he asked, noting that there was no one else near.

Suzannah smiled. 'Yes...again. You'll be thinking that I've invented my relations. My sister-in-law came back from Corner Brook last night, and as she's only here for the weekend I came out for the day to give them some space.'

'Ah, I see. So maybe when I've finished with my solicitor, as that's where I'm bound for, we could spend some time together?'

He looked so healthy and wholesome standing there, and so earnest in the manner of his request, that if she'd tried to say no she felt she would have choked on it.

So instead, throwing caution to the winds, she told him truthfully, 'I'd like that. I was envisaging a long, lonely day.'

If Lafe thought that she saw him merely as a repellent of boredom he gave no sign. 'Shall we say that we'll meet at this same spot in an hour?' he suggested.

'Yes,' she agreed, and with a smiling nod he went on his way.

So much for living the life of the 'man-less', Suzannah thought when he'd gone. Yet wasn't she presuming too much? He had merely suggested they spend some time together. That was all. He hadn't asked her to jump into bed with him. She could soon chill him off if the need arose.

When he came back Lafe was less relaxed than he'd been earlier. There was an expression on his face like that of someone who has just been hurt, and Suzannah wondered what his solicitor could have said to take the bounce out of him.

She was about to find out.

'I've known going to the dentist to be less painful than that,' he said as they strolled towards the store exit.

'Really?' she said sympathetically, and left it at that, deciding that if he wanted to tell her the reason for such a comment he would do so.

'I've just told my solicitor to sell my family home,' he explained, as if reading her thoughts, 'and it hurts. I've lived in the house all my life. But my father died suddenly a couple of weeks ago and I'm the only one of the family that's left.'

'So you're not married?'

He stared at her. 'No. Would you expect me to be here at this moment if I was?'

'No. I wouldn't, but there are lots of folk who would see nothing out of the ordinary in it.'

'Yes? Well, I'm not "lots of folk",' he said levelly.

Feeling that she'd been put in her place, Suzannah took up the conversation where they'd left off. 'And so you don't want to live there alone?'

'It isn't that,' Lafe said. 'I'm about to get involved in a project that needs a lot of time and energy. I love the old house and don't want to see it fall into disrepair.'

'But supposing you do get married. What then?'

'I don't know. I have to admit that I've always seen myself bringing up a family of my own there, but it seems crazy to keep the place on because of something that could be in the far distant future.'

'Where is it?'

'The house?'

'Yes.'

'Not far from Grenfell's abode. At the other side of the Curtis Memorial Hospital.'

He was eyeing her with a thoughtful blue gaze. 'Would you like to see it?'

'Oh, yes, I would,' she said immediately.

'Then let's go. I've walked here. Do you have your car?'

'No. I've left it at my brother's house.'

'It's no problem. We're only a matter of minutes away.'

As they strolled along the road that led to where the huge hospital stood at the bottom of the hill on the one side and the clear, cold blue of the Atlantic embraced the other, Lafe asked the question that had been eating at him ever since their meeting earlier in the week.

'Are you really here on holiday, Suzannah?' he asked. 'Or is there another reason?'

He saw her face close up and knew he'd hit a sore spot, but her voice was level enough as she told him, 'I was a doctor in an English hospital and was engaged to one of the consultants there, but something happened between us and I broke it off. I came here to get away from it all.'

As she watched his face lighten she thought guiltily that it was only part of the story, but the rest of it was her own affair.

'So, supposing a job became available here, how would you feel about that?'

She whirled round to face him and fixed him with astonished hazel eyes. 'You mean in health care?'

He was laughing at her expression. 'I certainly don't mean as a deep-sea fisherman.'

'I don't know,' she told him in continuing amazement. 'I've never given it a thought, but I suppose I might be persuaded.'

As they turned a bend in the road he pointed to a house standing on its own in a large wooded area, and Suzannah's eyes popped again, but this time for a different reason.

It was bigger than Grenfell's house, but like his, and ninety per cent of the rest of the houses she'd seen, it was made from wood. Also in common with the rest of them, it had the large basement area underneath that lifted the houses above the deep snow and ice that made up the Canadian winter.

This house wasn't a box, like some of them. It had grace and style. When he opened the front door and motioned for her to go in she saw that the inside was just as impressive as the outside, with beautiful polished wood everywhere and furnishings that spoke of wealth and good taste.

It took just seconds for Suzannah to know that if it had been she who'd lived here all her life it would break her heart to sell it.

'Don't do it!' she exclaimed, and as soon as the words were out she wished she'd kept quiet.

'Don't do what?'

'Sell the house. It's beautiful.'

'Was, maybe. It was all done to my mother's design, but Dad lived here on his own for some years after she died, and if you look closely there are many things that need doing.'

'So?'

'What? You think I should get them done...and keep it?'

She could feel her face starting to warm. Whatever had possessed her to start interfering in his life? For one thing, she hadn't known him five minutes, and for another she was acting like a normal human being, and she hadn't felt like one of those in a long time.

Lafe was shaking his head. 'No. I'm afraid that it will have to go. I have no need for a place as big as this and, much as it means to me, I've been away from it for most of the last few years.'

His smile had a whimsical sort of sadness about it. 'I'm a wanderer, Suzannah. As far as Canada is concerned at least. You name it, and I've been there. Hospitals in Vancouver, Halifax, Toronto. A two-year stint in the Arctic that's just come to an end, and now I'm about to sever the past for ever by selling the only true home I've ever known.'

He took a deep breath and Suzannah thought, What's coming now? I hope he's not going to ask me to show prospective buyers round!

She needn't have worried. It was something far more surprising that he was about to propose.

As she eyed him questioningly he said, 'I know of a temporary job that's available if you're interested. I get the impression that you're not in any rush to return to the UK, and if you want to work while you're here it would be ideal.'

'What is it?' she breathed, wondering where this strange conversation was leading.

'When they heard I was returning, the Western Health Care Corporation asked me to take charge of a new satellite clinic that they're opening in a few weeks' time. I've accepted and am going to need an assistant.

'It would be a temporary position to begin with as, although the health authorities have done this on a smaller scale in areas not quite so remote as the one they've chosen this time, they'll be monitoring it to see if it's worth putting extra strain on the budget with something of this kind. If you'd like to be considered I'll put your name forward to the powers that be.'

CHAPTER TWO

'How do you know that I'd be suitable? We haven't discussed my previous employment,' Suzannah croaked as astonishment tightened her vocal cords, and before he could reply she continued, 'And what do you mean by remote?'

Lafe's blue gaze had amusement in it. 'Which question do you want me to answer first? It's true that I don't know if you would be suitable from a medical point of view. Your hospital back home would have to come up with some answers regarding that. I'm just going on what I see.'

'And what do you see?'

'A beautiful English exile whose spark has been put out and awaits rekindling.'

She managed a laugh at that. 'Flattery will get you everywhere, but first tell me more about this place.'

'Have you heard of Port aux Basques, way down at the other end of the island?'

'Vaguely.'

'Well, there's an excellent health centre there with many facilities, but unfortunately it has to cover a very wide area. It's the only medical facility for many miles in south-west Newfoundland and has a catchment of thirteen thousand. That may not seem a lot to you, coming as you do from an overcrowded country, but in our sparsely populated land it's a huge number.

'In order to fulfil its purpose to the community the centre provides outpatient clinics in some areas, and the most recent project is the refurbishment of an old whaling station in one of the more remote areas to give the outlying communities a fair share of the health care they're entitled to.

'This is going to be bigger than anything attempted before, with two doctors *in situ* and four other staff. We're expecting to see patients from miles around. So, what do you think?'

'Thinking is what I'm going to have to do,' Suzannah said slowly with the amazement still upon her. 'I can't possibly give you an answer on the spot. There are other factors involved that I would have to consider.'

'Such as whether you want to work while you're here?'

She shook her head. 'No, not that. I'm drifting at the moment. Some kind of work would do me good, but…'

'But what, Suzannah?'

She ignored the probe. 'Leave it with me, Lafe. How soon do you have to know?'

'In a couple of days?'

'Fine. I'll be in touch…and now, having given me much food for thought, I must go and do my thinking.'

He nodded. 'Fair enough, and in the meantime I won't mention it to anyone until I hear from you.'

As she stood on the path, ready to leave, Suzannah looked up at the house. Behind it the sea glinted in the autumn sun. In front of it were trees, straight green conifers like guardsmen on parade, and in the middle was the place that had been home to Lafe Hilliard.

She had a feeling that his decision to sell came from reasons other than those he'd given her, and she would dearly like to know what they were, but for the present she had enough to think about.

When she told John and Debbie about the job offer it was her brother's turn to be astonished.

'Are you crazy?' he cried. 'I sincerely hope you told the fellow what he could do with his suggestion.'

'No, I didn't,' she said quietly. 'If it wasn't for the guilt that I carry around I would have taken the job straight away.'

'If it wasn't for the "guilt", as you describe it, you wouldn't be here in the first place! You wouldn't be considering moving to the wilds of Newfoundland with some guy you hardly know!' he exclaimed.

Always the voice of reason, Debbie had something to say.

'If Suzannah hadn't had the hiccup back home in England she wouldn't be here with us, as you so rightly say, John.

'And just think what that would have meant. We would have missed getting to know her. The boys adore their English auntie. So maybe some good has come out of it.'

She turned to Suzannah. 'If you want the job, take it. John is only fussing because he loves you.'

'I know.' Suzannah sighed. 'But it isn't that simple, is it? The authorities here will have to write to the hospital where I worked in England, and though I was eventually cleared of all blame we're all aware that mud sticks.'

Her face brightened. 'Maybe I could...'

'Could what?' John asked in a calmer voice.

'Get in touch with Malcolm Stennet, the clinical services manager. I imagine the enquiry would go to him, and if there's one person who stood by me when everyone else was having doubts, it was Malcolm. May I use your phone? I'll ring him at home.'

'Suzannah!' Malcolm Stennet cried when he heard her voice on the phone. 'I was beginning to think you'd disappeared off the face of the earth.'

'I'm staying with my brother in Newfoundland. Have been for the last six months,' she told him.

'I see. Then it's not surprising that no one has seen you lately. A certain person has been enquiring about you but, needless to say, I wouldn't have told him where you were even if I'd known.'

Suzannah felt her mouth go dry. 'Nigel?'

'Yes, the man himself. He's working in a London hospital now, I believe. Though how he got the position I really don't know after his slippery tactics down here.'

'Please, don't tell him where I am, Malcolm,' she begged.

The elderly manager chuckled at the other end of the line. 'I wouldn't give that scoundrel the time of day, least of all tell him where you are, and in any case Newfoundland is quite a large island. I wouldn't know where to direct him to.'

'You will when I've finished telling you why I've rung.'

'Fire away, then.'

'At the moment I'm living in St Anthony with my brother and his family, but I've been offered a position in health care in the Port aux Basques area of Newfoundland. I'd like to accept, but…'

'You're worried about that dreadful business that Nigel got you involved in?' he said as her voice trailed away.

'Yes, and if they discover what happened.'

'Suzannah, it's only your sense of guilt that's standing in your way. You were cleared, remember? So that information doesn't matter—it can't be used against you. It wasn't your fault and you have to stop punishing yourself. Take the job—I know you'll do brilliantly.'

'Bless you,' she said chokily. If it hadn't been for this man, the nightmare she'd found herself in all those months ago really would have torn her apart. But his faith in her and his calm common sense had helped her to keep a grip on her sanity and she would be forever grateful to him.

Nigel Summers was clever and ambitious. Too ambitious for his own good. Or, to put it more accurately, too ambitious for the good of the young registrar that he'd been engaged to.

They'd both worked on the paediatric unit of the hospital in the Midlands, he as senior physician and Suzannah in a less prestigious capacity.

He was quick-thinking, charming and a risk-taker. Nigel was also extremely arrogant. When they'd become involved in the dreadful episode that made her decide to give up medicine, he'd had no such scruples and had carried on working.

When she'd thought about it afterwards Suzannah had wondered what had attracted him to her. It certainly couldn't have been love on his part, or he wouldn't have tried to blame her for the mistake that he'd made in a moment of angry petulance.

Of a quieter and more cautious nature than he, she'd realised at the beginning of their relationship that a man like Nigel Summers didn't like competition. A wife with sparkle might have detracted from his own personality, but at that time it hadn't mattered.

Foolishly she'd let herself be caught up in the crowd of admirers that had always surrounded him, and when she'd got her breath back after his proposal she'd said yes.

If she'd seen the flaws in his personality, Suzannah had also admired his style and flair, and until the episode of the small daughter of one of the town's leading citizens being taken off a vital part of her treatment by him, for no other reason than he'd been annoyed, and Suzannah had questioned his judgement, the young doctor had been contented with her lot.

It had been on a dark November night that she'd had to call Nigel away from the dinner that he'd gone to with some golfing friends, and his expression when he'd come striding into the children's ward had said it all.

He'd had a few drinks and hadn't been pleased at being

called away from what had looked like being a boisterous evening.

'So why me?' he grated. 'It took me ages to find a taxi! Am I the only consultant in this place?'

'You're the head of Paediatrics, Nigel,' she protested tiredly. 'It's Hannah Kerwin in the side ward.' Knowing that he'd been impressed with the child's father's social standing, she added, 'You gave instructions that you were to be consulted about her treatment at all times.'

'So what's the problem?' he asked with the irritation still upon him.

Suzannah eyed him levelly. She'd been having second thoughts about her relationship with the hospital's high flyer for some time and this sort of episode didn't help.

It had been a very long day and she was exhausted. She should have been long gone herself, but various problems had cropped up to keep her there and now little Hannah was giving cause for concern.

The child was suffering from Reye's syndrome, thought to have been brought on by her having been given aspirin for a respiratory infection instead of the safer paracetamol.

It was a rare and serious condition. There was swelling of the brain and some liver damage, resulting in prolonged vomiting, memory loss and delirium, to name just a few of the symptoms.

For the liver damage she was having dialysis and for the problem with the brain she was on a corticosteroid drug, and until the last hour had seemed to be stable.

Her parents had been there most of the day and had just left when one of the nurses had come rushing to find Suzannah.

'Hannah seems to be in the throes of some kind of seizure,' she'd said, and the two women had hurried to her side.

The child had been having some sort of fit and despite

their efforts to stabilise her, and remembering Nigel's instructions, she had called him away from his dinner engagement.

By the time he'd got there Hannah had come out of it and that had added to his irritation.

'That kind of thing can happen with Reye's syndrome,' he said edgily as the two of them stood by the bed. 'Leave off the corticosteroid for the time being. The fit might have been a side effect.'

Suzannah looked up in alarm. 'Are you sure it's wise to do that?' she questioned with the feeling that he wasn't giving the matter his full attention. 'Hannah has been on it for quite some time and under the circumstances…'

His mouth tightened. Nigel wasn't used to having his instructions queried and he snapped, 'Why bother to call me out if you know better than I do? Just do as I say. Or, better still, as the end of your shift has been and gone, you can toddle off home. You're looking somewhat the worse for wear.'

Suzannah's colour rose. She'd been aware of the fact without Nigel commenting on it, and to make matters worse he was smiling at the young nurse who'd been assisting her before his arrival and saying, 'We'll take care of it, eh, Nurse?'

The girl, one of his admirers, and possibly envious of Suzannah's precarious relationship with him, glowed back at him, which made the tired young doctor give in to his seniority and her complete exhaustion.

'Very well,' she agreed. 'You're in charge. I'll do as you say.'

As she drove home Suzannah thought bleakly that this was how it would be if they ever married. A night out with his men friends would come before anything else. But at that moment she was too tired to contemplate it. Getting annoyed with him would achieve nothing. That one was a law unto himself.

She fell into bed when she got home, not bothering to set the alarm as she was off duty the following day.

When she presented herself back on the ward after her day off the first thing she saw was Hannah's empty bed and the same nurse who had raised the alarm a couple of days ago had averted her eyes from Suzannah's dismayed gaze.

That was the beginning of the nightmare. The nurse was saying that Suzannah had told her to cross the medication off the little girl's drug sheet and Nigel was denying having anything to do with it.

When she faced him with it he shrugged and said blandly, 'Am I likely to say such a thing? Any doctor worth his salt knows that it can be fatal to take a patient off a high dosage of that kind of drug. That they must be weaned off it gradually.'

'You're lying!' she cried. 'It was your suggestion, not mine. You weren't thinking straight. You'd been drinking and couldn't wait to get back to your friends. I questioned it and you sent me packing.'

'Do you really think anyone will take your word over mine, Dr Scott?' he said, not meeting her eyes, and in that moment she saw him in his true colours.

She stared at him coldly, determined not to panic. She knew she was innocent, but already a great weight of guilt had settled in her. If it had been an adult's life that had been lost it would have been bad enough, but for a child to be taken because of a doctor's carelessness didn't bear thinking about. And worst of all, because she hadn't insisted on staying to make sure Nigel didn't do what he'd suggested, that child had died.

When challenged by the authorities Suzannah maintained

her innocence, but such was Nigel's standing in the hospital that few believed her and there was no escape.

She had to face the distraught parents who were threatening to sue the hospital, the directors of the trust, the press. It had seemed as if every person she came across doubted her capabilities and integrity.

Needless to say, it was the end of the engagement. She couldn't even bear to look at Nigel. She'd been stupid enough to be taken in by his outward wrapping, without checking on the quality of the goods inside.

Malcolm Stennet stood up for her at the disciplinary hearing, pointing out that she'd been at the end of a twenty-four-hour shift and that Nigel Summers had come in from a dinner engagement where he had, no doubt, been drinking. He also brought to their notice Suzannah's exemplary service record.

Nigel did all that he could to pin the blame on her while appearing not to. He confirming that Suzannah had been at the end of a long and tiring day, and that maybe he hadn't made his wishes regarding the child's treatment as clear as he should have.

Suzannah couldn't believe it. He had some nerve. Whilst it seemed he was defending her, he made sure that everyone thought she was responsible.

But just when Suzannah thought her career was finished, the nurse who had been involved amazed her. Obviously afraid of losing her job, and perhaps realising that she'd been used, she admitted that she wasn't sure who'd told her to cross the corticosteroid medicine off the patient's drug sheet, and that it might have been Dr Summers as he'd sent Dr Scott home within minutes of his arrival.

Suzannah was cleared. There hadn't been a person on the panel who didn't smell something fishy on Nigel's part, but his excellent track record got him off with just a warning.

Her relief at being cleared was overwhelming, but the joy of working in health care had been wiped out. There was no way she wanted to carry on. A child that she'd been treating had died when she shouldn't have, and Suzannah had been on the fringe of it.

Whatever the verdict from the disciplinary hearing, it didn't stop her from feeling guilty and nothing was going to change that.

When John heard what had happened he invited her to stay for as long as she wanted, and the invitation came at just the right moment.

And now she'd met a man who had lit the flame again. He wanted her to work with him amongst his own folk. But what would Lafe say if he knew about her past? That she'd let an arrogant doctor who'd been drinking kill a child in her care?

She couldn't tell him. In spite of their brief acquaintance, she already knew that she wouldn't be able to bear him thinking badly of her...and supposing he retracted his offer?

But if he didn't find out before she started the job, she would tell him soon, she promised herself. When she'd proved that she was a good doctor...and an honest one.

According to Malcolm, Nigel had moved to a big London hospital. He had talent in plenty and would get to the top in spite of his failings. That was why he hadn't wanted to risk admitting that he'd given the wrong instructions.

Suzannah phoned Lafe on the morning of the following day to say that, subject to the Western Health Care Corporation's approval, she would like to be considered for the job.

'That's great, Suzannah,' Lafe said in his amiable Canadian drawl. 'Why don't we celebrate?'

She laughed at the suggestion. 'Wouldn't it be advisable to wait until we see if I'm accepted?'

'Why? We can celebrate again when that happens.'

'John and Debbie would like to meet you. She said to invite you round later for Sunday brunch if you're free. She'll be going back to Corner Brook in the early evening.'

'Big brother wants to look me over, does he?' he asked whimsically.

There was no point in denying it. John did want to meet the stranger who had strolled into her life and achieved what no one else had been able to.

Her brother could see that her lethargy had disappeared and it was this Lafe fellow who could lay claim to that. But apart from the fact that he came from one of St Anthony's oldest families, they knew nothing about him.

'Fine. I'd like that,' he was saying. 'What time shall I come...and where do they live?'

'Not a word to Lafe about what happened back home,' Suzannah told her brother as she and Debbie busied themselves in the kitchen.

Salt beef was on the brunch menu, a delicious moose stew, and sundaes made from bake apples, the apricot-coloured small berries that ranked as Newfoundland's most popular delicacy.

'As I've said before, mud sticks, and if it all comes apart for any reason, fair enough,' she went on. 'But in the event that it goes through I want to tell Lafe in my own time—when I've had the chance to prove myself. I don't want to start working with him with a cloud hanging over me.'

'Well, look at you!' John said with a grin. 'Haven't we become all determined and forward-looking since we met this roaming medic?'

Her face clouded. 'That might be how I seem on the outside, but it's all a front.'

She didn't tell him that if this chance to work with the man she'd met on Tea House Hill came to nothing, then she would be nothing, too. It would be a fitting end to the nightmare that had started when a tired doctor hadn't argued strongly enough against the instructions given by a senior colleague.

As Lafe enthralled the boys with tales of polar bears and the white wolves that roamed the Arctic wastes where he'd lived for so long, John followed Suzannah into the kitchen.

As she eyed him questioningly he gave the thumbs-up sign. 'So you don't think that Lafe will take me to his igloo and seduce me?' she teased, with a sudden vision of that smiling mouth on hers and his beautiful body arousing longings that she'd put on the shelf for ever.

John was smiling. 'He might take you to his igloo, but I'd like to bet that anything that goes on after that would be mutual.'

'Did I pass the test as far as your brother is concerned?' Lafe asked as she walked to his car with him late that afternoon.

'With flying colours.'

'And what about you?'

'What about me?'

'How do I rate with you?'

She could have told him that he was like a bright ray of light amongst the shadows of her life, that from the moment of meeting him he'd never been out of her thoughts, but wouldn't that be asking for trouble?

If her hopes didn't come tumbling down, they would be working together in a confined space if his description of the clinic and its situation were anything to go by.

So anything other than a business relationship would take some handling. She'd already had her fingers burnt with her ill-fated engagement to Nigel, the supreme egotist.

Personal relationships with colleagues were not a good idea.

Which made her answer his question with a sort of casual flippancy. 'I'll let you know, if and when we get the opportunity to work together.'

'That wasn't what I meant. I'm asking how you see me as a person.'

'Memorable.' It was a flattering description, but it could have meant anything.

He threw back his head and laughed.

'I give up. And in the meantime I'll speak to the powers that be and tell them I've found my assistant. Who do they get in touch with at the other end?'

'Malcolm Stennet, Clinical Services Manager.' She handed him a sheet of headed notepaper. 'The address of the hospital is on there.'

'Right,' he said easily. 'I'll be in touch once I know the score. I take it that you're available for interview if so required?'

She nodded, wondering what the 'score' would be. Would it be Suzannah Scott nil, Nigel Summers of the forked tongue the winner?

As he drove back to the house that would soon have a 'for sale' sign on it, Lafe's mind was awash with thoughts. The delightful English doctor he'd met beside Grenfell's memorial was treading carefully for some reason.

It had been obvious today in her manner, and he wondered why. Perhaps it was because in spite of their immediate rapport Suzannah was reminding herself that he was still a stranger.

Maybe she thought that after two years in the Arctic he would be sex-crazy, he thought with wry amusement. She wasn't to know that he'd gone out there on another escape trip and that it was only in recent days that the memory of Nicolette had begun to take a back seat in his mind.

Why that was, he couldn't be sure, but he knew that his pretty young sister wouldn't want him to mourn her for ever. That one day she would want him to put a stop to his restless wanderings and put down roots.

And was he going the right way about it? No! He was about to sell the house where they'd been brought up as cherished children. Where he'd expected to live one day with his own brood. Was he insane?

There were no repercussions from England and in the brief interview with the Newfoundland authorities that followed, Suzannah was told that the temporary position was hers.

She wasn't aware that Lafe had told them he wouldn't take the job if he didn't have her as deputy, but in the end there was no need for threats or cajoling. She got it on her own merits.

'So when do we start?' she asked when Lafe rang to give her the good news.

'As soon as the paperwork is sorted out with regard to work permits and the suchlike. Hopefully it can be done as soon as possible and we can be ready to begin as scheduled.'

'They're putting the finishing touches to the refurbishment of the old whaling station and it will start functioning on Monday next. Which means that we have to get settled in over the coming weekend.'

'Will all the equipment be *in situ* by then?'

'Yes. It's being installed now as we speak.'

'And is there enough accommodation for six staff?' she questioned.

'Yes, again. There are small cabins in the grounds for us. One for myself. One for you. And the other four staff will share the remaining two.'

'When you first described the place you said that it was remote,' she reminded him. 'Just how far off the beaten track is it?'

'Let's say that it's among a cluster of small communities in an area where the folk make their living from fishing. They're nearly all coastal villages where we're going, with just the odd motel, a store and sometimes a hall around which all their social life is centred. These folk have come a long way since Grenfell's day, but they're still not over-burdened with amenities such as full-scale health care.

'The authorities are aware of this and the project we are to be involved in will be similar to what he did all those years ago. But we'll be buzzing around in cars, not sledging with a dog team.'

'Is that why you've agreed to take part, because of Grenfell?' Suzannah asked curiously.

'Yes, in a way. Don't you feel the same compulsion?'

'Er…yes,' she murmured, but it wasn't strictly true. Yes, she felt the compulsion, but it was because Lafe Hilliard was involved…not so much in memory of Wilfred Grenfell.

It could have been awkward, her moving to the Port aux Basques area so quickly, because John and Debbie had been relying on her to pick up the boys from school each day. But fortunately Debbie had come home the previous weekend with the news that the promotion she was involved in was due to finish and normal mothering would be resumed.

'You'll be a long way from us in Port aux Basques, 'Zannah,' Richard had said when he found out that she was leaving. 'When will we see you again?'

'Soon, I hope,' she promised him.

She hid a smile when Robbie wheedled, 'Can we have extra stories each night until you go?'

'Yes, you can, my darlings,' she promised, and knew that she would miss her delightful nephews. But she'd been in their home long enough. It was time that John and Debbie had the house to themselves again.

Suzannah and Lafe left St Anthony in the early evening of Saturday. It wasn't a good time to start the long journey to the other end of the island, but someone had made an appointment to view Lafe's house and he'd felt that he wanted to be there.

'When I've shown them round I'll be able to tell by the way I feel whether I really do want to sell it,' he'd explained when he'd rung up to mention the late start.

'That's all right by me,' she'd said agreeably. 'As long as we get there before morning.'

'No worry on that score,' he'd promised, and so it was in the autumn dusk that they began the journey to Port aux Basques.

Suzannah had returned the hire car she'd been using and had bought herself a Jeep, with the thought in mind that if they were going to be moving around on rough terrain it would be more suitable than a car.

As she waved goodbye to John, Debbie and the boys and prepared to follow Lafe's Shogun, she had no idea how soon the Jeep's strength would be tested.

'Look out for the moose,' he'd said before they set off. 'They sleep during the day and come awake again in the evenings.'

She'd stared at him.

'So?'

'The woods at the sides of the road are full of them and sometimes they come blundering out into the path of the cars.'

'Really?'

He'd laughed at her obvious disbelief. 'Yes, really. The poor things are almost blind.'

They seemed to have been travelling for hours and, not having set eyes on a single moose, Suzannah was thinking that Lafe had been labouring the point somewhat. Then out it came, a big, dark shape with huge antlers, heading straight for the Jeep.

Desperately she swerved to avoid it and as the animal lumbered off Suzannah found herself in a ditch with her head crunched up against the steering-wheel.

'My God! Suzannah!' she heard Lafe cry from somewhere near. Then he was opening the door, his face stretched with concern. After making sure that she wasn't trapped anywhere, he eased her gently out onto the grass verge.

'Are you hurt?' he asked urgently in the dark night.

She shook her head and on a sob said, 'I don't think so, but I can't stop shaking.'

He cradled her to him and stroked her hair back from her white face and with his lips against her brow he soothed her into calm.

When she'd stopped trembling he said gently, 'I'm going to put you in the Shogun. We'll leave the Jeep here. I'll get a mechanic out first thing in the morning to get it back on the road and he can bring it to the clinic for you. Do you have any problems with that?'

She shook her head. 'No, of course not.' With a shaky laugh she said, 'It's going to look good if one of the doctors is the clinic's first patient.'

He kissed her damp brow again and, picking her up in his arms, said raggedly, 'You could have been killed! Thank God that moose didn't hurt itself or you.'

It was the first time they'd had physical contact of any kind, and in spite of being in shock Suzannah knew that she liked being held by Lafe and being kissed by him, even though it had been merely a gesture of comfort.

When he'd settled her into the passenger seat Lafe produced a tartan rug and proceeded to wrap it around her.

As she looked down onto his bent blond head she said softly, 'You're very kind.'

He looked up at that and he was smiling. 'Maybe I have some ulterior motives.'

'And what would they be?'

'That I feel guilty about what has happened because I'm the one who persuaded you to get involved in the Port aux Basques project. Also, because it's my fault that we're travelling at a time of day when the moose are around. If it hadn't been for the prospective buyer that I wanted to show round the house we would have been there by now.'

'And is that all?'

'Er...no...not exactly. You come over as very cool and efficient, someone who is quite capable of looking after herself under normal circumstances. So having you all weak and vulnerable is bringing out the best, or should I say worst, in me.'

He was laughing but she didn't join in. If Lafe knew just how inefficient she'd been on a never-to-be-forgotten occasion he would have to rearrange his opinion of her and she knew in that moment that she didn't want this man to ever think badly of her.

'And so what did your prospect think of the house?' she asked with a quick change of subject which he immediately latched onto.

'I notice that you're veering away from anything personal between us,' he said, and he wasn't laughing now. 'I get the message...and in answer to the question, they thought that it would be too big for their requirements.'

He didn't tell her how much it had hurt showing them round, especially when they'd gone into the room that had once been Nicolette's, and that he'd rung the Realtors and told them to put a hold on the sale for the time being.

It was clear that, like him, Suzannah had some sort of hang-up with the past. Or maybe it was the present. He didn't know. But, whatever it was, she should realise that few folk went through life unscarred.

His worst nightmares were always of the sea. The blue Atlantic that had taken his sister from him. When he'd dined with the English doctor and her family it had been like a knife in his heart as he'd watched brother and sister together.

There were times when he thought that his grief at the loss of his sister had taken such a slice out of his life that he'd missed out on marriage and family life because of it.

He'd gone from St Anthony, leaving his parents to grieve in their own way, and become a wanderer...a medical nomad who had only in recent weeks felt the urge to put down roots.

CHAPTER THREE

ALTHOUGH Suzannah had been agreeable to travelling late in the day she would have preferred to have arrived at their destination in daylight.

It wasn't the same, pulling up in darkness in front of what seemed to be a mere cluster of the wooden houses that the people of Newfoundland seemed to favour.

The only light was from the headlamps of the Shogun, and as she tried to make out the outlines of what was around them the thought came that Lafe hadn't been wrong when he'd described this place as remote.

A door opened at the nearest house and as light slanted across the bonnet an elderly woman appeared on the step.

'Guess you'll be the doctors,' she said as Lafe jumped down from the driving seat.

'That's right, ma'am,' he said. 'I'm Lafe Hilliard.' He indicated Suzannah, who was still inside the car. 'And this is Dr Scott. I notified the authorities at Port aux Basques that we were arriving today and was told that you would have the keys.'

'Sure do,' she said, dangling them from her fingers. 'The four separate ones are for the houses and the others are for the clinic.'

'I'm Maisie Roberts, representing the community council for these parts. You'll find the beds made up and food in the kitchens.' She pushed a straggle of white hair off her forehead. 'You're late. I'm off to my bed. If there's anything you folks are missing I'll be around in the morning. I do the janitor's job as well.'

She pointed to the dark outline of the hillside behind

them. 'Follow the road up the hill there and you'll come to the cabins.'

'Guess the brass band must have got tired of waiting and it was too dark for us to see the red carpet,' Lafe said wryly as he reversed the Shogun and pointed it towards the hillside.

'This is all my fault,' he went on with his usual good humour missing. 'I should have made sure that we arrived in daylight. You're all shaken up and we'll be having to grope our way around the place until we find the cabins.'

'It doesn't matter,' Suzannah said wearily. 'Just find me a bed to lie on and a cup of hot sweet tea and I'll be out like a light.'

It wasn't the moment to tell him that her neck was hurting. That she'd jarred it when the Jeep had gone into the ditch. Morning would be soon enough to inform him that he'd brought his first patient with him.

If the cabins looked basic from the outside, the interiors were a pleasant surprise. They were immaculate, with comfortable furniture, polished wooden floors and newly fitted kitchens. All of which was making Suzannah feel more cheerful.

'Which one do you want?' Lafe asked.

'The one next to yours,' she said immediately. 'Just in case I get a visit from any local wildlife in the night, such as moose, caribou...or the odd polar bear.'

He laughed. 'This isn't Ice Station Mercury where I did see one or two polar bears, and the caribou are more likely to be found on Labrador, but moose there are in plenty. Though they're harmless enough. They're the hunted rather than the hunter.'

When they'd each chosen their accommodation Lafe made tea in Suzannah's kitchen, and as they sat one at each side of the table he said, 'I hate to be the harbinger of bad news, but you have a black eye that's in a class of its own from when your face hit the steering-wheel.'

She groaned. What a start! Tomorrow she would be wearing a surgical collar if one could be found, and with a black eye to go with it she was going to stand out in the crowd.

Yet where was a crowd likely to come from in this place? It was on the cards that she and the man who was watching her thoughtfully over the rim of the mug that he was drinking from were going to be bored out of their minds in this backwoods.

The health-care people must have had their reasons for choosing the site, but at that moment they were totally obscure.

'Welcome to Bramble Bay,' Lafe said softly, as if guessing her thoughts. 'I hope that you're not a movie fanatic or a nightclubber, Suzannah, as it will be a long ride if you are. Something tells me that we'll have to make our own amusement out here.'

What was that supposed to mean? she wondered. There was a challenge in the bright blue gaze meeting hers and, remembering how much she'd appreciated being held in his arms beside the deserted road just a short time ago, she told herself that she was crazy, coming to a place as remote as this with a man as desirable as Lafe Hilliard.

He was on his feet and tuning into her thoughts again.

'Don't worry about it, Suzannah. Lock your door when I've gone and get a good night's sleep. We'll breakfast together here, eh?'

'Yes, please,' she told him as the depressing aspects of Bramble Bay receded with the promise of breakfast with the Viking.

For a second Suzannah couldn't think where she was when she awoke in a room full of sunlight, then it all came back.

The moose coming towards her out of the trees, Lafe holding her close until she'd calmed down, and then arriving at what had looked like the last outpost of civilisation in the early hours of the morning.

As she moved her head on the pillow her neck hurt. She'd felt it a few times during the night but had been too tired to let it break into her sleep, but now there was no ignoring the pain.

Getting carefully out of bed, she went over to the window and the sight that met her eyes made her gasp. The cluster of houses they'd pulled up in front of the night before stood squat and clean in the morning sun, and there were others like them dotted along the coast for as far as the eye could see.

Running alongside them was a sandy shore with fishing boats scattered around, and beyond it, glittering blue and breath-taking, the Atlantic.

A small white church stood farther along the waterfront and she thought that no matter how small, how remote the community, there was always a place to worship.

As Suzannah looked farther afield she was amazed to see the bulky outline of a factory of some sort on the distant skyline. Maybe it belonged to the English paper firm who long ago had seen that Newfoundland was an island covered in trees, and so had established themselves, long term, on the island.

Bramble Bay was beautiful, she thought. At that moment nothing moved. In the quiet of early morning the place sparkled tranquilly beneath the autumn sun, and the cinemas and nightclubs that Lafe had mentioned could have been on another planet for what need she had of them.

But where was the clinic?

A knock on the door had her reaching for a robe, and when she opened it Lafe was there. 'Am I too soon?' he asked, eyeing her tangled chestnut mop and the hastily thrown-on robe.

She shook her head. 'No. I'm starving. I've just been admiring the view. This is a much nicer place in the daylight.'

'Tell me about it!' he said with feeling. 'I've been doing the same as yourself, wallowing in the morning glory of the place, and it dawned on me eventually that I couldn't see the clinic.'

'I was thinking the same.'

'Exactly. A disused whaling station shouldn't be that hard to pick out.'

'And?'

'I've decided that it must be at the other side of this rockface that our cabins are next to. So when we've eaten I suggest we go in search of the Bramble Bay Clinic. We've got just one day to get ourselves acclimatised.'

He was watching her as she walked in front of him to the kitchen and after a moment he said, 'What's with the neck?'

'I jarred it when the car went into the ditch.'

'Let me see.'

She came to a halt in front of him and Lafe carefully felt all round her neck. 'Everything seems to be in its right position,' he told her, 'but you've obviously pulled the muscles, and if there's one thing I don't carry around with me it's a surgical collar.'

'Maybe we'll find one in the clinic, although I'd imagine that car accidents are rare in these parts. If you remember, we hardly saw another vehicle as we drove here. Which reminds me, I must ask our friend Maisie Roberts if she knows a mechanic who can sort out your car and bring it here.'

'Yes,' she agreed absently.

The Jeep was the last thing on her mind at that moment.

The touch of those large capable hands on the slender stem of her neck and the smooth tops of her shoulders was something that she'd wanted to go on for ever. But she couldn't risk getting involved again.

If she was going to start wilting every time Lafe touched her she was going to be a pushover, just like she'd been with the treacherous Nigel, and that would mean that she'd learnt nothing from her past experiences.

He was looking at her with puzzled eyes and Suzannah felt ashamed for comparing this man with her ex-fiancé. So far he was turning out to be everything that Nigel was not.

But she wasn't ready for another relationship with anyone—not until she could come to terms with Nigel's betrayal and deal with the guilt that constantly tormented her. Then came the question which haunted her the most—what would Lafe think if he ever found out why she'd left England?

Lafe was putting bacon under the grill and when it started to sizzle he began to cut into the big crusty loaf that had been left for them the night before. Bringing her thoughts back to the present, Suzannah started to lay the table.

When they sat down to eat he said, 'And what was going through your mind a few moments ago?'

She looked up, startled that he'd noticed and was asking for answers.

'Er...nothing...really,' she hedged, with a gut feeling that *his* past would be as white as snow.

'You were back in England, weren't you?' he persisted. 'I can always tell when your thoughts are back there. Are you still in love with your English doctor?'

She shuddered. 'Far from it. The thought of him makes my skin crawl.'

That had him eyeing her in bemused surprise. 'Then what is it that hurts so much?'

Deciding that attack was the best means of defence, she said flatly, 'I don't pry into your private life, Lafe, so will you, please, not poke your nose into mine?'

'Sure,' he answered coolly, 'but I have to warn you that I don't care for working with staff who have mental hang-ups that they aren't prepared to bring out into the open.'

If she'd been controlled before, she wasn't now. 'I'm no different now than when you asked me to apply for the job,' she snapped, 'and you weren't passing judgement then. So why now?'

'I'm not passing judgement,' he said, reverting back to his usual easy manner, which infuriated her even more. 'It's just that I feel I'm not seeing the real you.'

'Maybe,' she replied with the anger still in her. 'But as far as I'm concerned, what you see is what you get!'

What his answer to that would have been she didn't know as the sound of footsteps outside on the path broke into the conversation.

It was Maisie Roberts of the night before, looking much more amenable in the light of day.

'Everything all right?' she asked when Suzannah invited her inside.

If she noticed that the lady doctor wasn't dressed, and that they were breakfasting together, she gave no sign, but Suzannah had to overcome a strong urge to tell her that they'd spent the night apart, as they would be doing every other night in Bramble Bay.

And that she'd found them like this because it was their first morning in the place. But something told her it would sound as if she were trying to justify herself too much...and why, for heaven's sake, should she have to do that? She and Lafe were here to work and that would be it—subject to their services being required.

According to the paperwork that Lafe found waiting for him when they let themselves into the clinic, their back-up staff were to consist of two nurses, one male, one female, a receptionist and a physiotherapist.

The sprawling wooden building was like their accommodation, basic on the outside but impressive within. There was a comfortable waiting room with outside telephones for the use of patients, a consulting room for whichever doctor was seeing them, alongside a nurse's room with all modern facilities and, impressive to say the least, a small pharmacy that would be manned by a series of relief chemists.

Lafe nodded approvingly at that and commented, 'It's no good giving a sick person a prescription if they have to travel miles to get it made up.'

He saw her doubtful expression and said, 'I can tell that you're still of the mind that we'll be twiddling our thumbs most of the time, but remember there's a factory not too far away and, although Newfoundland is sparsely populated compared to England, there are more people living in these remote areas than you would think.'

'Surely the factory will have its own medical centre,' she'd said.

'I'm sure that it will,' Lafe had agreed, 'but the employees might need us at times when they're not working.'

She was eyeing him questioningly. 'So are we to be a twenty-four-hour service?'

Lafe shook his head. 'No, of course not, but we're bound to be called out for emergencies that aren't too big for us to deal with. Obviously any really big catastrophes will be covered by the Port aux Basques people.'

He was checking through the medical supplies as he spoke and seconds later he turned to her with a triumphant grin. 'One surgical collar, Dr Scott, if you would like to come forward.' As he placed it carefully around her neck and then bent to tie it at the back, Lafe brushed her smooth skin with his lips.

There was nothing suggestive in the gesture. She knew that. It was merely his way of saying, You're all fixed up now. But it brought her round slowly to face him and it was as their eyes met that the moment changed.

The bright blue of his gaze had darkened. His lips had parted as if in slow wonder, and to her astonishment Suzannah found that it was she who was reaching out for him, taking him into her arms.

After the first moment of being rooted to the spot he came alive and Suzannah discovered that Nigel's patronising embraces were as nothing compared to the warmth and passion in Lafe Hilliard. She was drowning in it and longing for more.

But after being the one to make the first move, she was also the one to bring the moment of madness to an end. 'We can't...' she gasped, pushing him away. 'We mustn't! Maisie is somewhere around, for one thing...'

'And for another...?' he said with dangerous calm. 'There's got to be another. You wouldn't spoil it just because our elderly janitor is in the vicinity.'

'I was going to say that it isn't ethical,' she muttered lamely. 'It never works when medical staff start that kind of thing.'

'What kind of thing?' he asked with the deadly calm still upon him.

Her fighting spirit was returning. 'Don't pretend you don't know what I mean, Lafe. Remember I've already tried it once.'

'And was it as good?'

'No. It wasn't,' she told him with reluctant honesty. 'But it makes no difference. I can't stand the thought of making another mistake.'

'You have some nerve, Suzannah,' Lafe said with a rage of his own kindling. 'Just how short is your memory? You were the one to make the first move.'

Her face was burning. 'Yes, I know, and I'm sorry. It's a pity that you aren't more difficult to get on with... and less attractive.'

He was smiling for the first time during the war of words.

'And that's your excuse, is it?'

'Yes, that's my excuse,' she agreed, and as the phone on the desk beside them began to ring she left Lafe to answer it and prepared to beat a swift retreat.

'It's John for you,' he called, halting her hasty departure. After passing the instrument to her, it was his chance to put some space between them, striding out of the small consulting room with the easy confidence that was so much a part of him.

'You arrived safely, then?' were her brother's first words when he heard her voice.

'Yes, everything is fine,' she fibbed.

John would only start fussing if she mentioned the moose incident, even though he would be well aware that such happenings did occur.

Were she to tell him that she'd just thrown herself into Lafe Hilliard's arms and was now wishing she hadn't, he would be likely to fuss even more, but she wasn't going to do that, was she? The only two people who were going to know about that moment of insanity were the two participants.

Three of the staff and the rota pharmacist would be reporting for duty on Monday morning as they were coming from Port aux Basques, but Linda Strachen, the female half of the two nurses, appeared in the middle of Sunday afternoon.

When Suzannah saw the long-legged redhead getting out of a smart car at the front of the clinic and witnessed the woman's reaction to Lafe when he went out to greet her, she decided that with that sort of style and confidence she had to be one of the directors of the health corporation that had organised this venture.

But when they came inside, with Lafe carrying two large suitcases and the new arrival following with various other baggage, she was surprised to find on being introduced that she was one of the nurses, one of the team that they'd been allocated for the running of the clinic.

'You're a patient quick to take advantage, I presume,' Linda Strachen said before Lafe could explain Suzannah's function in the clinic.

It was annoying to be so categorised on such short acquaintance, but she supposed that the surgical collar and the black eye weren't exactly what the woman would be expecting to see on the second in command.

'No, I'm not, as a matter of fact,' she told her coolly. 'I'm Dr Suzannah Scott, Lafe's assistant, and my injuries are because he makes a practice of beating up his staff every time they step out of line.'

In the silence that followed Suzannah couldn't believe what she'd just said, but how dared the woman start patronising her the moment she'd set foot in the clinic?

Lafe was eyeing her with a sort of chiding amusement and the new nurse, after being momentarily disconcerted, gave a throaty laugh.

'I understand you, Dr Scott.' Then she went on, as if a matter of no consequence had been dealt with, 'I'd like to see where I'm going to be staying. It's been a long drive.'

'From where?' Lafe questioned with his easy smile.

'St Johns. I've been working in one of the hospitals there and decided I was ready for a change. I didn't realise that this place was so far away from civilisation, though.'

Calculating green eyes were looking him over, and to Suzannah's annoyance Linda Strachen came out with the same kind of comment that he'd made earlier.

'Guess we'll have to make our own amusement.'

'My sentiments exactly,' Lafe said smoothly, picking up her cases. 'If you'd like to come this way I'll show you where your cabin is.'

In the months that Suzannah had been in Newfoundland she'd been amazed how quickly the weather changed on the island, and during the night that followed there was further proof of it.

In the late evening of what had been a mild, sunny day, the temperature dropped to zero, and when she got out of bed the next morning to face her first day in the clinic she was amazed to see a thick covering of snow outside.

John and Debbie had warned her of the severity of the winters, that they were long and very cold and how for months on end the roads and pavements were covered in snow and ice. Yet she hadn't expected it so soon.

Thankfully she'd come prepared with warm boots and the right kind of jacket, and there were a couple of skidoos parked round the back of the clinic so that if moving around on the snow became difficult the motorised toboggans would be there to assist.

But she wanted the mellow autumn to persist. She'd met Lafe on a day in late September when the ferns had turned to gold and the leaves had been changing to the paler greens and bronzes of the season, and somehow it was significant of their relationship. A warm, golden thing that, she had to admit, was meaning more to her every day.

Maybe the morning's reminder of the sharp chill of winter had come to bring her to her senses, because there'd been nothing sensible about the way she'd behaved the previous day.

And with thoughts of yesterday in mind there had to be the memory of the patronising Linda Strachen. She could only hope that the remoteness of the clinic and the early snow might drive her back to St Johns.

When the cocksure nurse had talked about making their own entertainment the predatory green eyes had fastened on Lafe, and Suzannah knew that he'd got the message. Would he send out signals of his own?

She would be devastated if he did. Yet who was she to be agonising at the thought? She'd told him to keep out of her life. So what right had she to interfere in his?

When she looked up he was there, standing knee deep in the snow outside his cabin, his face ruddy from the cold and a pale sun glinting on his short golden crop. She caught her breath. He was magnificent, this doctor who was just as warm as the ice and snow that he was accustomed to was cold.

It was incredible that he wasn't married. A man like Lafe would be noticed wherever he went. But from his own words he was a wanderer. How long would he stay in this place? One thing was clear in her mind. If he didn't stay long, neither would she. Bramble Bay would only be bearable with him around.

The soft thud of a snowball on the window told her that she'd been observed, and when she waved he called across, 'Welcome to winter wonderland!'

Suzannah smiled. No one would have guessed from his carefree stance that the new venture he was to be in charge of was about to commence in just over an hour.

Maybe he was of the same opinion as her, that they were going to be out on a limb here. She was accustomed to the bustle of a busy hospital, and from what Lafe had said he wasn't used to being idle either.

Carefree though he might appear, there had been nothing slapdash about the way he'd gone over the place yesterday. Premises, paperwork, amenities both inside and outside the clinic, had all been thoroughly vetted, and by the time he'd finished he'd had the brusque Maisie eating out of his hand.

When it came to yesterday's new arrival it hadn't been

easy to tell who was going to be eating out of whose hand during those first few moments of acquaintance, but Suzannah didn't have happy feelings about Linda Strachen.

Time alone would tell whether her instincts were right as, living here in the wilds of Newfoundland, the staff would all be thrown into each other's company a lot more than in normal health-care circumstances.

Lafe was looking at his watch. 'One hour to blast-off!' he called across, and Suzannah nodded. He was ready for action and she was still in her nightdress. A shower followed by a quick breakfast was called for, and then...what?

The first day was over and it had been chaotic, with staff adjusting to new routines and new surroundings and, as Lafe had described it, everybody from miles around coming to be treated for something, from ingrowing toenails to a suspected heart attack.

'Where on earth did they all come from?' Suzannah said dazedly when the last patient had gone and the staff were assembled in the small admin office.

'These areas are deceptive,' Alison Jones, the receptionist, said. 'The places may look to be sparsely populated but it's misleading. The houses are widely spaced because there's so much land available, which gives the impression that not many live in the district.'

She and her husband, Wayne, who was the other nurse appointed by the corporation, had come from Port aux Basques and still hadn't unpacked their belongings.

They would be sharing the last unoccupied cabin, and Shirley McAndrews, the rather staid physiotherapist, was to have the pleasure of the company of the redoubtable Linda.

'Come back, Florence Nightingale! All is forgiven,' Wayne Jones had said to his wife in a low-voiced aside when the glamorous nurse had glided into their midst just minutes before the clinic had opened.

A dour man of few words, he was just as unlikely a candidate to be nursing the sick as she was, but as the day had progressed Suzannah had seen no cause to doubt their efficiency.

Especially Linda's. She wasn't compassionate or caring. Intimidating would be a better word, but she knew what she was about and Suzannah had to admit that in a crisis she would be a valuable asset.

'Thank you all for a memorable first day,' Lafe said, 'which I think has shown us why we've been put here. I suppose it might be the novelty of it or curiosity which has brought everyone out in the first snow of the winter. Tomorrow we could be surplus to requirements but, whatever the reason for today's packed waiting room, it's clear that we have a purpose to serve in this place.

'When you've all eaten and had a chance to unwind, I'd like you to come over to my place for a celebratory drink.'

At one point during the day Suzannah had questioned the wisdom of those who lived beside this isolated part of the coast, by saying to Maisie Roberts, 'There are so many amenities in places like St Anthony and Corner Brook, especially in health care. Yet these people choose to live here.'

The elderly Newfoundlander had smiled. 'What you don't realise, Doctor, is that there are many of us who prefer the old way of life, hunting the moose and caribou, fishing on our own doorsteps and gathering the berries.'

'You'll have seen the bake apples that are such a popular treat here? Well, they're found where it's swampy and it's only the likes of us who know where to look.'

'And as to medicine, don't think we're not grateful to have you folks here, but I can remember my mammy using the juice from the gum tree to stick my scalp back together when I got caught with an axe when I was small, as there wasn't no doctors or hospitals in those days.'

'Did the treatment work?' she'd asked doubtfully.

'Sure did. Never had a second's trouble with it. There's a mark there, of course, but that's all there is to see.'

And now, as Suzannah cooked herself a meal in the cabin's small kitchen, it was the modern medicine of today that was occupying her mind.

A young child had been brought in with severe abdominal pains. Her stomach had been tender when touched, and as the discomfort was localised mainly in the lower right-hand side of the abdomen, both Lafe and herself had suspected appendicitis.

The mother, whose round, flat features and straight black hair spoke of Inuit descent, had listened impassively as they'd explained what they suspected and had told her that the girl was going to need hospital treatment, possibly an operation.

'She needs to be taken there as quickly as possible,' Lafe explained, 'as if the appendix is allowed to burst there could be a risk of peritonitis.'

'Do you have transport?' Suzannah questioned, and in case the answer was no she was about to pick up the phone to call an ambulance. But the woman surprised her, however, by pointing to an expensive estate car on the clinic forecourt.

Linda Strachen was wrapping the child in a blanket and as Lafe swung her up in his arms and prepared to follow the monosyllabic mother to the car, he said in a low voice, 'If we'd been desperate we could have always commandeered the school bus, with the ambulance station being at Port aux Basques, but...' with a nod in the direction of the vehicle '...one should always expect the unexpected.'

An elderly man from the cottage next to Maisie's was

another one of the patients they saw. He was suffering from muscle pain in the arm and shoulder.

'He's spent the last two weeks chopping up logs that he's had given him,' Maisie said when she saw him in the waiting room.

'And now he's done himself harm. I told him he should have waited until his son came.'

'Do you think it's Maisie that should be sitting behind the desk?' Lafe said laughingly when she'd gone bustling off.

The last patient of the day was the most serious and when Suzannah finished examining her she went to find Lafe.

'I think we have a case of septicaemia,' she said soberly. 'Will you come and have a look?'

She'd found him in the kitchen, having a coffee with Linda Strachen, but he put down his cup immediately and followed her into the consulting room.

The fifty-year-old woman had presented herself with a hugely inflamed and swollen face, so much so that the outlines of her features had disappeared into what looked like a bright red blob.

Suzannah heard Lafe's quick intake of breath and knew that he was as alarmed as she at the patient's condition.

'How long have you been like this?' he asked gravely.

'My face started to swell two days ago, but I thought it was an allergy as I'd been eating a few things that I'm not used to,' she informed him.

'Is it painful?'

'Not my face, but my neck hurts.' She swallowed hard. 'It's serious, isn't it? What is it, Doctor?'

'We think that you've got some form of septicaemia, but where that kind of infection invariably attacks the whole system, in your case it's concentrated around your face and head. I'd like to consult with my colleague for a moment if you'll excuse us.' He ushered Suzannah into the outer office. 'What do you think it is?' he asked quickly. 'Whatever it is, there's no time to waste. She needs antibiotics and plenty of them, or it could be fatal.'

'It's definitely a septic infection,' Suzannah said, 'but why only her face?'

'I'm putting my money on erysipelas,' he muttered. 'It's a serious streptococcal infection but, unlike septicaemia, it's confined to just that part of the body.'

'I've heard of it, but never seen it before,' she told him.

'That's because it's very rare,' he explained. 'It can come from the tiniest scratch or graze, or maybe a bite, but when it gets hold, well, you've seen for yourself, haven't you?

'We'd better get back to the patient. We have to get her hospitalised with all speed and this time, whether she has her own transport or not, we need an ambulance in case she worsens before we can get her some treatment.'

Later in the evening they were going to phone Port aux Basques to enquire if Lafe's diagnosis had been correct and to enquire about the patient's condition.

And as Suzannah went to her wardrobe to find something suitable to wear for Lafe's drinks party, she was still bemused to think that they'd been faced with an illness so rare on their first day at Bramble Bay.

CHAPTER FOUR

IF HAVING a suspected case of erysipelas on their first day at Bramble Bay had seemed bizarre, so did the gathering in Lafe's cabin later that night.

Brought together in a common cause, it didn't alter the fact that they were strangers, although with every day that went past Suzannah was having to admit to herself that it felt as if she'd known Lafe Hilliard all her life.

Yet she hadn't, had she? Their acquaintance covered only a matter of weeks, but what weeks they'd been! In a short space of time he'd turned her life round, brought her out of the doldrums of guilt and disenchantment and given her new impetus.

Maybe he had that effect on everyone he met, she thought, and his staff would be just as mesmerised as she was, when they got to know him better.

The husband and wife, Alison and Wayne Jones, were sitting quietly together, sipping home-made ginger cordial which had been Maisie's contribution to the evening. In complete contrast, the luscious Linda was downing dry white wine as if there was no tomorrow.

As the physiotherapist, Shirley McAndrews, eyed her apprehensively, Suzannah thought that here was someone who wasn't delirious with joy at the prospect of sharing a cabin with the cocksure nurse.

The physio who, according to her records, was in her early forties and unmarried, was a quiet, rather plain woman, whose only claim to beauty was the clear, pale skin characteristic of the ash blonde. Sadly, the combination of the two did give her a rather washed-out look, and compared to the vibrant redhead she was like a nervous ghost.

Suzannah wasn't the only one taking note of Shirley's unease. Drawing her to one side, Lafe said, 'I don't think it's going to work out, Linda and Shirley sharing a cabin. How would you fancy having Linda with you?'

'No way!' she exclaimed angrily. 'That one is too full of her own importance.'

'She knows the job, though.'

'I should hope she does. And in case you haven't noticed, so do the rest of us!'

'What?'

'Know what we're doing.'

'Did anyone say that you didn't?' he asked levelly. 'I was merely trying to establish the best possible harmony between us all. Shirley isn't the only one not happy about the pairing off. Linda has already had a word with me and that was why I thought that you and she would make a better combination.'

'Look, Lafe,' Suzannah said, with the irritation still upon her, 'there are times when I can't even stand my own company, let alone that of someone like Linda.'

'So the answer is still no?'

'Yes, it is, and don't make it sound as if I'm being unreasonable.'

'So you don't feel that you are?'

'No. I don't. If you're so concerned about harmony, why don't you offer to let Linda share with you? I'm sure it would be right up her street. She'd bite your hand off.'

If she'd been hoping to needle him, it didn't work. He was laughing as he exclaimed, 'What! And have Maisie having a heart attack?'

He turned away, serious again. 'It's plain to see that I've rubbed you up the wrong way and I'm sorry. Let's forget it, shall we?'

'I'd be prepared to share with Shirley,' she said quietly. 'I could cope with that. Even though I would prefer to be on my own.'

He swung back to face her. 'Great. That solves the problem all round. I'm sure that our shy physio will be happy with that arrangement.'

'And Linda will be smug because she's got a place to herself...where the rest of us can't see what she gets up to,' Suzannah pointed out.

'And what would you expect that to be?'

'Having seen the way she looks at you, I think you can work it out for yourself.'

He was watching her consideringly with his bright blue gaze. 'You're tired...and your neck's hurting, isn't it?'

'Yes, it is, and, yes, I am tired. And you think that's why I won't share with someone who's as different from me as chalk from cheese?'

'This isn't how I visualised us spending our first evening as a team,' he said in a low voice. 'Perk up, please, Suzannah, while I go to tell Shirley the good news.'

In the end it did turn out to be a pleasant occasion. Shirley came over to say how much she appreciated Suzannah's offer of sharing. Alison and her solemn husband began to unwind, with no credit to the ginger cordial, and Lafe was his usual unflappable self.

Only Linda struck a sour note as she continued to drink steadily, and Suzannah couldn't help but notice that Lafe was the only one who wasn't showing disapproval.

'Will Nurse Strachen be fit to attend to the patients in the morning?' Maisie asked as she was leaving.

Suzannah's heart missed a beat. The last thing Lafe needed was for word to get around that one of his staff had a drink problem.

'Yes, I'm sure she will. It's first-night nerves, I would

imagine,' she replied with a convincing smile as Linda draped herself around Lafe on the couch.

'Hmm. Maybe,' the elderly woman said doubtfully, adding, 'There's a lot of drinking goes on in these parts as there's not much else to do. Especially the men. They'll be coming in with their liver problems. You'll see.'

'Right. So I've that to look forward to, have I...amongst other things?' Suzannah remarked laughingly.

Alison and Wayne had disappeared by this time. Shirley had gone to transfer her belongings and Linda was asleep on the couch, which left Lafe and Suzannah with a moment to themselves.

'So, what do you think?' he asked.

'About what?'

He shrugged broad shoulders. 'Everything.'

Not to be drawn, she said, 'Ask me in a couple of weeks' time. At the moment I'm in the process of adjusting to Bramble Bay.'

'So you're not so sure?'

'No. I like it. It's different from any other kind of health care, but—'

He groaned. 'There's always a but.'

'I don't think I could stand it if you weren't here.'

'So we're friends again, are we?'

She smiled, and with her glance on the recumbent Linda, who was snoring softly, told him, 'Only if you carry that one back to her cabin. I've made the supreme sacrifice on her behalf and Shirley's. Linda's got a place to herself now, so that's where she should be sleeping.'

It had been said teasingly, but Suzannah knew she couldn't bear the thought of them both spending the night in his cabin. She was jealous! Jealous over a man she was determined not to fall in love with.

He bent and swooped the limp figure of the nurse into his arms. 'No sooner said than done, Dr Scott. Don't go.

I'll be back in a second. There's something I want you to see.'

Lafe was as good as his word. 'I've laid her on the bed and covered her with a warm blanket,' he said. 'She shouldn't come to any harm, but I wouldn't like to have her headache in the morning.'

With the feeling that Linda Strachen had monopolised enough of the evening with her affairs, Suzannah questioned, 'So what do you have to show me?'

He took her hand and led her into the kitchen. The blinds were up and he pointed to where the skidoos were parked. 'Yours, madam, I believe.'

As her eyes took in the dark shape of the vehicle beside them she cried, 'My Jeep! They've rescued it.'

'Sure have. Believe it or not, there's a garage just down the road. I phoned them and they went out for it straight away.'

'I owe you a lot, Lafe,' she said gravely. 'You've done so much for me since I met you, and what do I do? The first time you ask me to do something for you, I refuse. I'm so sorry.'

Her voice had thickened as she fought back remorseful tears. 'Hey,' he said gently, putting his arms around her. 'What's all this about? All I've done is find you a job and get your Jeep back.'

Suzannah looked up at him with the memory of past pain in her eyes. 'You've done much more than that. When I met you I was living in a dark limbo...and now I feel that I'm in the light.'

Touching his tanned cheek gently, she whispered, 'I only wish the demons would go away.'

'We all have skeletons in our cupboards and that's the best place for them,' Lafe said gently. 'Life is for living, Suzannah, and you might be surprised to know that I've only recently come to that conclusion.'

'I don't believe it,' she said wonderingly. 'You're the most positive person I've ever met.'

'Don't be deceived,' he said with a far-away look in his eyes. 'My young sister was drowned some years ago in circumstances that I still can't bear to talk about. For a long time after that I was like a piece of flotsam drifting from job to job, place to place. I still am to some degree, but of recent months I've got my thoughts in line. For the first time in years I know where I'm heading. So, you see, I'm far from being a positive thinker.

'One thing I am tuned in to, though. It's past midnight and we have another long day ahead of us tomorrow. I'll walk you to your cabin...and I do hope that you won't find it too irksome, having to share.'

Suzannah pulled a wry face. 'Don't remind me of my ingratitude, please! I'm sure that Shirley and I will get on famously. I'll do my best to make her feel at home. As you said before, she's shy...and rather nervous.'

He laughed. 'Unlike a certain person that I've just had to carry to her cabin.'

'Exactly,' she agreed lightly, while admitting to herself that the thought of Linda being held in his arms wasn't a pleasing one.

She was moving towards the door and he put out a restraining hand. 'Do you want to hang on for a moment while I phone to enquire about our patient with the septic face?'

'Yes, of course,' she said immediately. 'That was some infection. I hope they've caught it in time.'

When Lafe came off the phone he was smiling. 'I've just spoken to the night sister. It was erysipelas. She says that the lady is being given massive doses of antibiotics intravenously and, though as yet there is no improvement, her condition hasn't worsened any, which makes me think that they've managed to arrest the infection.'

'Thank goodness for that,' she breathed. 'And while gratitude is on the menu, thanks again for having the Jeep brought in. And now I really must go.'

As she stepped out into the cold night her feet shot from under her on the icy path and down she went into a thick patch of snow. Feeling totally foolish, she lay there, looking up at him in the light of a winter moon.

'You all right?' he asked anxiously as he bent over her.

'Mmm,' she murmured. 'That's the good thing about falling on snow...it's soft.'

Lafe's arms were reaching out to her. 'And what about your neck? That little tumble won't have done it any good.'

'It doesn't seem any worse,' she said in the same abstracted tone. 'The only thing I'm aware of at this moment are these...' And she rested her hands on his forearms.

'Do you want me to let you go?' he questioned gently.

'No,' Suzannah told him insanely.

'Then maybe the moment calls for something more progressive...like this,' he breathed, lifting her to her feet.

It was there again, the magic that was Lafe Hilliard. His kisses were long and searching, his arms the haven that she'd ached for. But she'd forgotten that the cabins were only feet apart, and when a door clicked open Suzannah pushed him away.

He didn't demur, just smiled and let her go. Feeling oddly deflated, she slithered across to her own front door and wished him a brief goodnight.

Shirley had made up the spare bed and was already asleep, so there was no need to discuss anything until the morning. Still dazed at the way a slip in the snow had escalated into passion, she ran to the window to get a last glimpse of Lafe before he went into his own cabin.

But it wasn't his own place that he was entering. Lafe was going into Linda's lodgings, and when half an hour passed without him leaving, Suzannah was forced to come to the conclusion that it didn't take that long for him to check if someone who'd had too much to drink was all right.

Maybe when he'd referred to making their own entertainment he'd seen himself as the clinic stud, she thought bleakly as she threw back the covers of her empty bed. Going from one to the other with his easy charm.

The next morning started with an accident. Lafe received a call from the motorway police to say that a big truck carrying logs from a timber yard on the other side of Port aux Basques had swerved in high winds and deposited part of what had obviously been an insecure load onto a passing car.

'We've sent for ambulances,' he was told, 'but it will be a while before they get here and the authorities at the other end said for us to bring you folks out while we're waiting, as you're the nearest.'

'I have another doctor and one nurse available,' Lafe told him. 'We'll be on our way in seconds.'

He'd yawned a few times since coming on duty and Suzannah had eyed him coldly. Obviously he'd had a busy night. The sultry Linda looked pale and heavy-eyed, too, whether from the effects of her hangover…or leg-over, she wasn't sure.

But they both threw off their lassitude when the call came through and, as Lafe had promised, the two doctors were on their way in seconds, with Linda to assist and Wayne holding the fort at the clinic.

There'd been four people in the car. A six-year-old boy had escaped injury, but his parents and grandfather had been badly injured, the older man being the worst.

From the looks of it, he and the boy had been on the back seat and he'd thrown himself over the child to protect him, but in so doing he'd taken the full brunt of the lorry's load as it had come through the roof of the car.

They'd been able to drag the boy from underneath him but the old man was still in the car, unconscious under a pile of logs that were protruding through the gaping hole in the roof.

'We couldn't risk moving him,' one of the traffic police at the scene said. 'It needs the fire brigade and the paramedics to do that.'

'Heads are going to roll for this,' he said grimly to anyone who was prepared to listen. 'Fortunately we'd been following the truck for the last couple of miles, otherwise we wouldn't have been on the scene so quickly. There's always a risk with these sorts of loads in high winds. We could see the logs had shifted and were just about to flag him down when it happened.'

Lafe was weighing up the state of the car. 'I need to get inside to see if he's still breathing,' he said urgently.

'Wouldn't risk it if I were you,' the policeman said. 'Not until the fire brigade get here anyway.'

Lafe shook his head. 'I have to get to him now. If there's no pulse I'll have to try resuscitation somehow or other.'

He turned to Suzannah, who'd been listening with dread in her heart. 'You attend to the others, Dr Scott. There's only room for one of us in here...if that.'

'Then let me go in,' she said quickly, elbowing him out of the way. 'I'm smaller than you.'

'No way!' he snapped. 'I'm in charge. Just do as you're told.'

'But supposing the car catches fire while you're inside,' she pleaded.

He was already throwing off his heavy winter jacket to reduce his bulk. 'Then it will be me that goes up in smoke rather than you.'

As he eased himself carefully inside the wrecked car

Suzannah obeyed his instructions. The trapped man wasn't the only victim of the dreadful accident, and as she ran across to where Linda was attending to the younger couple the nurse made known her findings.

'We've got head injuries and broken bones here, Dr Scott. The head, upper arms and shoulders have taken most of the impact, but both are conscious.'

'Where's Andrew?' the injured woman moaned. 'My son.'

'He's safe and sitting in the police car,' Suzannah told her gently.

'And my dad?'

'He's still in your car. We don't want to move him until the ambulance services get here. Dr Hilliard is with him and won't leave him until they get here.'

Suzannah felt sick every time she thought about Lafe crouched beside the injured man. If anything happened to him... What would she do? How would she feel?

She'd be devastated, totally, because she was in love with him. Disillusioned though she might be with life in general, there was no way that she was going to make herself believe that she wasn't in love with Lafe Hilliard. And if she was heading for further heartbreak, the fates would be to blame for throwing her into his path.

Even as the chaotic jumble of thoughts was racing through her mind she was examining the injured man and woman with deft, experienced hands and checking their vision and pulse rates, reminding herself as she did so that their well-being was more important than her affairs. She'd let personal problems, along with complete exhaustion, divert her attention once before, with disastrous results, and no way was it ever going to happen again.

As the sound of approaching sirens came nearer, Suzannah let out a sigh of relief. Help was at hand! The staff of the clinic in the wilderness would soon be able to return to their own small health centre.

They watched sombrely as the severely injured man was freed from the car by a fire crew, whilst others dealt with the leaking petrol all around. As the ambulance drew away to make way for a second one that would take the victim's daughter and son-in-law to the same hospital, Lafe said, 'There was a pulse, but it was getting fainter. The old guy will be lucky if he pulls through.'

'We're taking the boy to join up with his grandmother at the hospital,' one of the traffic police said. 'She's been informed of the accident and is on her way there.'

The two doctors nodded their agreement. The child needed to be with his own folks and the mother needed to see for herself that he was safe. As for the boy's grandad, he had acted with the protective instinct of the elderly for the young, and they could only hope that he would pull through.

Driving back to the clinic, Linda was quick to sit beside Lafe in the front of the Shogun, leaving Suzannah to occupy the back seat.

If he noticed the manoeuvre he gave no sign and chatted about this and that to the now perky nurse until they pulled up on the forecourt of the converted whaling station.

It was covered with small trucks, Jeeps and the odd motorised toboggan, but with the natural good humour of the Newfoundlander the owners weren't complaining about being kept waiting.

Alison had informed them of the accident and most of them had settled down with stolid resignation to await the return of the doctors.

'You look distracted,' Lafe said as they took off their outdoor clothes before presenting themselves to the patients. 'What's wrong? If it's the argument we had about who was taking responsibility for the man in the car, you surely didn't think I would let you take that risk while I was around to do the honours?'

Suzannah shook her head. 'No! Of course it isn't that.' And with a recklessness that she couldn't believe she was capable of, she said, 'I'm bemused by your conduct in general.'

'Meaning?'

'You spent the night with Linda, didn't you? Not content with mesmerising me with your attentions, you'd no sooner left me than you were going into her cabin. It's small wonder that you were yawning your head off this morning and she was all pale and interesting.'

'Huh!' he snorted. 'So that's why you're trying to equal the weather for lack of warmth. Thanks for the vote of confidence. You'll have to keep an eye on me, won't you? It might be my intention to seduce the shy Shirley tonight, or snuggle in between the Jones couple... or, then again, I might come calling on you. I suppose it's only fair that I should spread it around.'

He was angry, a new emotion for Lafe, and Suzannah didn't like him in this mood. But who was to blame for that?

She was. Because she was jealous. It had been a painful moment when she'd admitted to herself that she loved him, but now that she'd faced what was in her heart, where did she go from here? Not back into Lafe's arms every time he beckoned. That was for sure!

Why couldn't she have met an old man with a stick up on the hillside above Grenfell's house on that never-to-be-forgotten autumn day? Or somebody who was nondescript and ugly, instead of Lafe Hilliard, the roving medic, with eyes as blue as the watchful sea and hair like English corn.

'You can mock as much as you like,' she said stonily. 'But I thought you'd come out here to treat the sick, not to set up a harem.'

He was laughing now, the anger gone, and it made her feel even more dejected.

'Come on, Suzannah,' he said. 'Our patients have waited long enough. I'll take you up on the harem comment some other time.'

'Isn't Dr Hilliard great to work with?' Shirley said as she and Suzannah ate together that evening.

'Yes, he is,' she agreed with reluctant sincerity. The day had gone well in spite of its late start. Amongst those filling the waiting room there'd been the usual coughs and colds, a grossly overweight man with a heart condition who'd needed serious counselling with regard to adopting a stricter dieting procedure, followed by a woman in her fifties who was menstruating so heavily that a hysterectomy was almost certainly going to be needed, subject to investigation by the hospital.

And now it was time to unwind…if it were possible.

Suzannah was still coming to terms with the fact that she'd fallen in love again so soon after her disastrous engagement to Nigel.

Was she the sort of person who was unable to resist any man who showed an interest in her? she wondered as she toyed with the food on her plate.

It was a foolish question. The way she felt about Lafe had shown her how wrong her relationship with the English paediatric consultant had been. She'd been young and gullible when he'd snared her into his net, but she'd grown up a lot since then and one of the things she'd learnt had been not to be too hasty in placing her trust in others.

Was last night a reminder of that? Lafe going to Linda straight from her own arms?

As they washed up after the meal there was a knock on the door, and when Suzannah went to answer it the pushy nurse was on the step.

'Can I come in?' she said. 'I'm bored and I'm looking for company.'

'Why don't you take up where you left off with Lafe?' Suzannah said coolly.

Linda pulled a wry face. 'Don't mention it. He came in to check on me and found me about to choke on my own vomit. The poor guy sat with me for the rest of the night.'

So that was it, Suzannah thought dismally. She ought to have known better than to jump to conclusions like she had. No wonder Lafe had been miffed.

What a start it had been for him! His second in command sustaining a neck injury and a black eye on the way there. Then one of the nurses drinking to such an extent that he'd been afraid to leave her alone. And through it all he'd been his usual good-tempered self. Until she'd spoken out of turn.

Which all went to show that she was still on a self-inflicted disaster course when it came to the opposite sex. Obviously an apology was called for, and she hoped she could make it without giving away how she felt about him. But after her display of petty jealousy he'd probably put two and two together and made four.

'I have to pop out for a moment,' she told the other two women. 'I've left my purse at the clinic.'

Lafe's cabin was in darkness but the Shogun was parked nearby so he had to be somewhere around and the obvious place was the clinic. But that was also in darkness and Suzannah stood, irresolute, wondering where to look next.

Her eyes went to the snow-covered hillside behind the buildings, and it was then that she saw him, standing motionless on the slope, the dark shape of him silhouetted against the winter skyline.

And to complete the cameo that was essentially Newfoundland, a member of the moose population was just a few feet away from him, the huge antlers and dark bulk of the myopic beast complementing the stance of the man.

When she called his name he turned and came slowly down the hillside towards her. As he drew nearer she could see his expression and there was no joy in it.

'What's wrong?' they asked of each other simultaneously, and that brought a glimmer of a smile to his face.

'You first,' she told him, hoping that it wasn't their earlier skirmish that had put his light out.

'The old man trapped in the car died on the operating table,' he said flatly. 'I rang the hospital a few minutes ago.' He gave a frustrated sigh. 'If we could have moved him I might have been of some use. As it was, the only thing I was good for was monitoring his pulse and giving him a painkilling injection when he showed signs of coming round.'

'His injuries were very serious, Lafe,' Suzannah said gently. 'And his position in the back seat of the car made it virtually impossible for you to do any more than you did. These things happen. Acts of God that seem to have no rhyme or reason.'

'I suppose so,' he agreed glumly as they fell into step. 'But it doesn't make it any less frustrating from a doctor's point of view. The only good thing to come out of it is that he saved the boy.'

'Yes, he did,' she said. 'He gave his life for his nearest and dearest.'

'Indeed, yes,' he agreed heavily, and Suzannah had a strange feeling that she'd just hit a nerve.

'What did you want me for?' Lafe asked as they approached the back of the clinic.

'Shirley and I have got a visitor.'

'Oh, yes. Who?'

'Linda, and she explained why you stayed the night in her cabin. I do apologise for my display of childish pique.'

If she'd expected a response of any kind she was to be disappointed. Lafe's thoughts were in some far-away place.

He merely nodded and said briefly, 'Forget it, Suzannah. I have.'

So she could have saved her breath for all the impact the apology had brought forth, she thought despondently. If she'd wanted to know just how much she figured in his scheme of things, she'd just had her answer.

'There was *some* good news from the hospital,' he said as they stopped outside her cabin.

'What was that?' she asked quietly, with the feeling that Lafe was ready to talk about everything under the sun except themselves.

'The boy's parents are out of danger...and while I was on the line I enquired about our erysipelas patient again. She's doing well. The antibiotics are reducing the infection. It seems as if the danger is past.'

'That's good. I hope that someone has warned her that she's almost certain to get thrush after such huge doses, but thank goodness everything isn't doom and gloom,' Suzannah said, dredging up a smile.

Loth to leave him in such uncharacteristically low spirits she offered, 'Why don't you come and have a nightcap with us before you turn in?'

He shook his head, but for a moment his bounce was back as he said with a smile of his own, 'I might be tempted to get into the same state as Linda was yesterday, and then it could be your turn to play night nurse.'

'It was coffee or a hot chocolate that was on offer, not a trip to the off-licence—if there is such a thing in these parts,' she informed him lightly. 'So, you see, you wouldn't have been at risk.'

'Oh, no?' he parried in doubtful amusement as he opened his door. 'Some other time maybe. I wouldn't be very good company tonight...and I do have some sleep to catch up on.'

CHAPTER FIVE

IN THE days that followed, Suzannah often found herself smiling at the comparison between the huge brick structure of the hospital where she'd worked in England and the collection of one-storey wooden buildings that made up the satellite clinic.

The only similarities between the two was that they were both staffed by capable members of the medical profession and were both engaged in treating the sick, a function the same the world over.

Her relationship with Lafe was the thing that mattered most in those early days. If she was having to be content with it being that of one doctor towards another, she accepted it and was relieved up to a point that it hadn't veered into anything more personal.

Not so the attitude of Linda. With her predatory confidence she was out to make him notice her, whether he wanted to or not. As Suzannah watched him keep her at arm's length with his smiling good humour she wondered how long it would be before matters came to a head in that direction. Linda wasn't the type to be put off if she set her sights on someone or something, but neither was Lafe the type of man to be manipulated.

Suzannah often wondered what exactly it was about his sister's death that had put such a blight on his life...that had turned him into a medical nomad. Grief was a natural thing, but time was also a great healer. It looked as if there were aspects of the tragedy that were still very painful in spite of it having happened some years ago.

After that first night when they'd gathered in Lafe's

cabin for a get-together the staff had gone their separate ways when off duty.

Alison and Wayne Jones kept to themselves on the cold winter evenings, as did Suzannah and Shirley most of the time, but they couldn't help noticing that Linda wasn't happy with her own company and if she could wangle her way into Lafe's orbit she would.

There was a motel on the bend of Bramble Bay. That, and the small community hall, were the places where the locals gathered to socialise, and if the staff of the clinic felt the need to do likewise they would go to whichever of the two places offered the best entertainment.

Suzannah had found the Newfoundlanders a pleasant, uncomplicated sort of people, who lacked the sophistication of some of the more developed countries but made up for it with a sort of homespun integrity.

It was easy enough to believe that life on the island had been hard in bygone days. There had been little industry to support them and the Newfoundlanders had been forced to rely on the sea and wildlife for survival.

That way of life still applied in remote areas such as Bramble Bay, and for someone from England it was fascinating to watch.

In the days when Wilfred Grenfell had arrived in Newfoundland poverty had been widespread, and Suzannah wondered if the warm welcome they'd received from the people could be compared to the joy that he must have been greeted with.

The surgeries weren't as packed as on those first few days, but there were still a fair number of patients waiting patiently to be seen when they opened up each morning.

On a cold morning in late November they had to dig themselves out of the snow around the cabins to get across to the clinic. Rosy-cheeked and breathless, Suzannah was in the process of removing her heavy boots when a call came through to say that hunters, emerging from the nearby forest, had found an unconscious man slumped over the wheel of his car at the roadside.

'We're bringing him to your place, as you're the closest health centre,' the voice at the other end of the phone said.

'Good job they came across him. It's cold enough to freeze to death out there,' Lafe said as they waited for them to arrive. 'Though I'm not sure that they wouldn't have been better taking him straight to Port aux Basques. If surgery should be required or laboratory tests, that's where he needs to be.'

When a truck pulled onto the snow-covered forecourt they went out together, and Suzannah saw that the man was lying on his side in the back of the vehicle covered in blankets.

He had his back to them, but there was something familiar about the stylishly cut brown hair and the shape of his head. As she stared at him, almost hypnotised, Suzannah felt as if the ground were rocking beneath her feet.

It wasn't! It couldn't be! Not out here in the wilds of Newfoundland, she thought incredulously. But as she bent over him she already knew that it was so. Nigel was here in Bramble Bay!

How and why she didn't know, but she'd never been more dumbstruck in her life.

Lafe hadn't seen her colour drain away or how she was swaying on her feet. He was bending over the still figure in the truck and asking as he did so, 'Were there any signs of injury, or any other person present?'

The men who'd brought him in answered no to both questions and he said briefly, 'Let's get him inside, then, before he dies of hypothermia.'

They carried the limp form into the clinic and laid him on the couch in the consulting room, and if Lafe noticed that Suzannah was hanging back and that she was deathly pale, he made no comment. He just eyed her keenly for a moment and then turned his attention to the unconscious man.

'This guy is carrying a rash,' he said soberly as he examined him, 'and if I'm not mistaken it's the one that goes with bacterial meningitis. He's going to need a lumbar puncture and blood tests, but first we have to get him to hospital where those things are available...and we need to do it quickly.'

'Ambulance?' Suzannah croaked, with the strange feeling of unreality still upon her.

'Yes. Phone for one immediately, and while you're doing it I'm going to risk it and give him some antibiotics intravenously, as I'm pretty sure I'm right about the meningitis.'

He was raking his golden crop with fraught fingers. 'We can't risk transporting him ourselves. It's too contagious. Though, God knows, it would be quicker.'

When she came back after making an urgent request for an ambulance Lafe's eyes flicked over her briefly. 'Are you all right? You look as if you've seen a ghost.'

Suzannah managed a smile. No way was she going to tell Lafe that this was the man who'd taken the joy out of living as far as she was concerned. If she did, the rest of it would have to come out and he might not want her working with him when he'd heard the full story of what had happened back in England.

'No. I'm fine,' she lied. 'It's just that one never knows from one minute to the next what is going to happen in this place.'

Lafe was frowning. 'I won't dispute that. Have you been vaccinated against meningitis?'

'Yes, back in England when there were some cases admitted to the paediatric unit. What about you?'

'I've had the jab, too, but the guys who brought him in

won't have had it. As yet we haven't got a stock of the vaccine here so they'll have to drive into Port aux Basques.'

The man on the bed began to moan at that moment, and the two doctors could tell that the pain of the meningococcal infection was penetrating his unconsciousness.

Lafe glanced at him anxiously and then transferred his gaze to his watch. 'Come on!' he urged to the absent paramedics, adding to Suzannah, 'We both know that time is of the essence in cases of this sort. If they don't hurry we're going to lose him.'

The hunters had gone, protesting grumpily about the need for the vaccine but nevertheless prepared to drive into the town to get it, and twenty minutes after their departure the ambulance came screeching onto the forecourt of the clinic.

When it had gone, with the noise of its sirens breaking into a grey afternoon, Suzannah sank onto the nearest chair and asked herself the questions that she'd had to push away in the urgency of the moment.

If Nigel had been on his way to see her, and there was no other reason she could think of for the suave consultant to be in backwoods such as this, why was it? What was he doing here?

Obviously he'd been taken ill on the freeway and, knowing the speed with which meningitis could strike, the fact that he'd been found slumped in his car was easy enough to accept.

It was his presence in Newfoundland that was so hard to believe. If he'd been seeking her out for some reason, how had he known where to find her?

Only John, Debbie and Malcolm, back in England, knew where she was and none of them would have told Nigel of her whereabouts. Yet he'd been travelling in her direction and now he was gravely ill. So many questions, but no answers were forthcoming.

If there was one person she wouldn't have expected to arrive on her doorstep in a thousand years, it was Nigel Summers. The mere sight of him, helpless though he had been, had brought back the nightmare of those weeks and months when she'd carried the burden of the guilt of both of them. And as she'd once told Lafe, the thought of him made her skin crawl.

But he'd been taken ill, seriously so, in a strange country, and as the only person known to him the least she could do was go to see him at the first opportunity.

'Any news on the meningitis patient?' she asked casually as they cleared up at the end of the day.

'I haven't had a chance to ask,' Lafe said. 'Maybe you'd like to check with the Port aux Basques people.'

'Yes, of course,' she said quietly, while noting that Linda was hovering around him like a bee with a honey-pot.

'The lumbar puncture shows meningitis, as you suspected,' Suzannah told him when she came back. 'He's on massive antibiotics and is beginning to regain consciousness.'

'Do we have a name?' Lafe wanted to know.

'Er...yes. The men who found him handed in his wallet.'

'And?'

'He's an English doctor by the name of Nigel Summers.'

Lafe smiled. 'English, eh? It would have been strange if you'd known him.'

'Yes, wouldn't it?'

Desperate to change the topic, she went on, 'If you'll excuse me, I need to get back to my cabin. It's my brother's birthday today and I want to ring him.'

'Yes, of course,' he said. 'And, Suzannah...'

'Yes?'

'Take the morning off tomorrow. You look as if you could do with some rest. You're not sickening for something, are you?'

If an unwelcome face from the past was sickening for something...yes, she was, she thought dismally, and again the question came to mind. Why was he here? What was Nigel doing in Canada?

If it had been Toronto...yes. The place had style and a charisma of its own. With the huge expanse of Lake Ontario cuddling up to it, it was a great place to visit, whereas Bramble Bay and the far-flung Port aux Basques were the last kind of places to attract the sophisticated consultant who was a coward at heart.

'No. I don't feel as if I'm going down with anything,' she told Lafe quickly, but, grasping the opportunity that he was offering, she said, 'I wouldn't mind a few hours to myself, though. Thanks for the offer.'

'And what about me?' Linda said from the doorway. 'Don't I get any time off?'

Lafe laughed and ruffled her hair as he passed. 'No, 'fraid not. I like to keep you where I can see you.'

And exactly what that had meant Suzannah would have very much liked to know.

Shirley rolled over sleepily as Suzannah opened the cabin door at six o'clock the next morning.

'What's the matter? Have we overslept?' the physiotherapist mumbled.

Suzannah put her finger to her lips. 'No,' she whispered. 'I've got an errand to do. Don't tell Lafe. He's given me the morning off, so let him think I'm having a lie-in.'

'There's more snow forecast. Take care,' the other woman warned drowsily, and went back to sleep.

The treatment was working. Nigel was backing away from death's door, but he was still seriously ill. That was the message Suzannah received when she presented herself outside the isolation ward where he'd been placed.

'May I see him?' she asked of the sister. 'I've had the vaccination.'

'Are you a relative?'

'Er, no, but I'm an acquaintance. I doubt whether he has any relatives in Newfoundland.'

'Yes, well, just for a few moments, then. Mr Summers is conscious now. The people at our satellite clinic at Bramble Bay probably saved his life by administering antibiotics before he was brought here.'

She smoothed invisible creases out of a starched apron and went on to say, 'He's still very weak so, please, don't tire him.'

Suzannah nodded, grateful that the sister hadn't asked for more details about herself. The last thing she wanted was for the woman to find out that one of the doctors from that same clinic was known to the sick man.

It looked as if Nigel was going to get better, she thought as she approached the bed. For that she was thankful, but her gratitude stopped there.

Having to make this clandestine visit was distasteful to her. She was deceiving Lafe and hated doing it, but she had to find out what Nigel was doing here.

And when it came to the deception, why was she only worrying now? She'd been deceiving Lafe all along by accepting his job offer as if she were whiter than white, when she'd had one of the biggest black marks against her that a doctor could have.

The man she'd once thought herself to be in love with was lying on his back with his eyes closed, but when she said his name in a flat monotone he opened them.

'Suzannah!' he breathed. 'What are you doing here?'

'It's what are *you* doing here?' she hissed angrily.

'Looking for you, of course.'

'And why would you be doing that?'

'To say I'm sorry.'

'Huh! I'll bet. You're here because you want something. How did you know where to find me?'

A grimace of a smile crossed Nigel's face. 'I have friends in low places.'

'They don't come any lower than the place you left me in. You're a liar and a coward.'

He ignored that. 'Malcolm Stennet's typist gave me the info after she'd typed the letter to the health authority at Port aux Basques. It was then that I found out where you were hiding.'

'I'm not hiding,' she said in a furious whisper. 'I've nothing to hide from. Malcolm will have me back any time I'm ready. *So why are you here?*'

'I've told you, to say I'm sorry. I made a mistake…we both did, but I left you to face it.'

'You did me a favour,' she told him coldly. 'You taught me never to put my trust in anyone but myself, and nothing has changed. So get back to where you've come from, Nigel. I left England never wanting to see you again and I haven't changed my mind.'

His eyes narrowed. 'I want you back, Suzannah. I can still make it look bad for you with the authorities here.'

He might be weak and ill but the mocking smile that she'd grown to detest was playing around his mouth.

'A dead child to account for…and you would expect them to understand?'

In that moment Suzannah knew that the only understanding that mattered was that of Lafe. She'd told Nigel that his treatment of her had destroyed her trust in others, but it wasn't strictly true. In Lafe she'd found a man like no other, a man that she would trust with her life, but what would he think of her if he ever discovered her secret?

A rustle of skirts and the sister was beside her. 'You must leave now, I'm afraid,' she said. 'The patient isn't well enough for prolonged conversation.'

Suzannah nodded. She couldn't argue with that, but he'd been well enough to threaten her, which was typical of Nigel. If he'd been dying he would still have had something to say that would blight her life.

As she drove home it was becoming clear that she'd made matters worse by showing herself to him. Yet wouldn't he have got in touch with the clinic if she hadn't? After all, he'd known where to find her and only a deadly infection had prevented him from turning up.

Maybe she could have introduced him to Linda if he had, she thought with a grim smile. Those two would make a good pair.

It was early afternoon when she got back, and the first person she saw was Lafe, talking to a man with the unmistakable features of the Inuit. The man was holding a basket of freshly caught fish, and as she got out of the car he handed two plump cod to the golden-haired doctor and then, with an odd little bow, hurried off.

'What was all that about?' she asked, bracing herself for reciprocal questioning.

He laughed and her taut nerve ends slackened. 'A gift from a satisfied customer.'

Lafe was swinging the fish gently to and fro on the hook from which they were hanging, and as she watched them hypnotically he said, 'There's too much here for me. How about me making you dinner tonight?'

Suzannah hesitated. It was a very tempting offer, but did she want to be in his company, just the two of them for that length of time? When the day's duties were over she wanted time to think, to adjust to the threat that Nigel presented and to work out a way to prevent him from destroying her happiness here with the man she loved. Because love him she did, and nothing was ever going to change that.

'Tomorrow, maybe,' she said with a smile. 'They'll keep until then, and if you do the main course I'll do the starters and dessert.'

'Why are you putting it off?' he surprised her by saying. 'Not anything to do with you having been to Port aux Basques, is it?'

Suzannah felt her colour drain away. 'How do you know where I've been?'

'I rang up to enquire about the fellow brought in by the hunters, and the nurse who answered the phone told me he'd had a visitor that sounded very much like you.'

'Yes, it was me,' Suzannah said, sticking to the truth as far as possible. 'I'd gone there to do some shopping and decided to follow up his admission to the hospital for myself. I was just about to tell you that I'd seen him. He's going to pull through. You got a pat on the back from the sister because you were so quick to start treating him. He probably owes his life to you.'

Did Lafe believe her? she wondered. It seemed that he did as, with the fish still swinging grotesquely from the hook, he began to move towards the door.

'So tomorrow it is?' he questioned as she took her white coat off the peg and thrust her arms into the sleeves.

'Yes...and before you go, what's been happening while I've been away?'

He pretended to think. 'Er...Linda seduced me in the snow and Shirley has promised to do the Highland fling the next time we all have a get-together.'

I love you, Lafe, she thought. I love your beautiful body, your kind eyes, your mouth that once took me to paradise, and last, but not least, your skills, which are wasted here in the backwoods.

'I was asking about our patients—not the goings-on of the staff.'

'Ah, the patients. Now, let me see. Oh, yes. The wife of

the fellow who owns the motel came in with a scalded hand and Mrs Fosgate, the leader of the Women's Institute, had to be passed on to Port aux Basques with a broken wrist.

'Apart from those two, it's just been the usual run-of-the-mill things. Like a spate of young chickenpox sufferers, which means that we're likely to have shingles following on in some of their elders.'

'But tell me, before I take these two fellows to my fridge, how were your brother and his family back in St Anthony when you rang?'

'Fine,' Suzannah said easily. They were on safe ground now. Just as long as he didn't ask what they'd talked about. Nigel had been the main topic and when John had heard that he was in Newfoundland he'd been horrified.

'How did he manage to discover where you were?' he'd asked.

'I don't know,' she'd told him, 'but I intend to find out.' And she had, to the extent of learning about a breach of confidentiality at her old hospital.

But none of that mattered now. It was too late to do anything about it. What did matter was that she shouldn't be separated from Lafe.

Later that night, as she lay sleepless beneath the planked ceiling of the cabin, it seemed a definite possibility. Only Nigel would have had the nerve to seek her out as he had, then calmly suggest they take up where they'd left off. If he discovered that she was in love with someone else he would spoil it just for spite.

John had asked if Lafe had received any offers for his house and it had brought to mind that day when he'd taken her to see his family home and, unable to help herself, she'd told him not to sell.

She hadn't been in love with him then, but something had made her say it, and now the nearest thing to heaven that she could imagine would be to live there with him as his wife.

But Lafe was a free spirit. He'd confessed to being a wanderer, a man who had no wish to put down roots, and those kind didn't go in for matrimony.

The question isn't likely to arise, she told herself glumly. When Lafe finds out about your questionable past he won't touch you with a bargepole, and find out he will if Nigel tunes in to the situation.

But Nigel is too ill to do much meddling at the moment, she reminded herself as sleep at last began to tug at her eyelids. And if he doesn't come here to Bramble Bay, you'll be spared.

Spared for how long, though? Scandal has long arms.

The cod, straight from the cold waters of the Atlantic, with fresh crunchy vegetables and a cheese sauce, was delicious. As was the pavlova that Suzannah had made with the help of a whisk borrowed from Maisie and a foray around the sparsely filled shelves of the small store beside the headland.

She'd discarded the businesslike shirts and trousers she wore for work and chosen the most attractive dress she'd brought with her for the meal with Lafe. Calf-length, with a scooped-out neckline and three-quarter sleeves, it was made out of a heavy cream brocade that made the dark chestnut of her hair glow bronze in the light of the lamps and turned her skin to smooth ivory.

Anything less suitable for a meal in a log cabin miles away from anywhere would have been hard to find, but Suzannah didn't care. If everything between them fell apart in the very near future, she wanted Lafe to remember her as she was tonight, beautiful, desirable, tempting...

It was having the desired effect. From the moment of opening the door to her he'd been bemused. As he took the pavlova from her, his eyes told her that he liked what he saw and it wasn't the meringue that was having that effect.

During the meal they talked of all things except themselves—including a remark from Lafe to the effect that the mystery English doctor was still on the mend. It was a comment that made Suzannah's heart beat faster for a few moments until the magic took over again.

The condemned woman ate a hearty meal, she thought wryly as they got up from the table, and prayed that the executioner might have a slow recovery.

As she started to clear away, Lafe shook his head. 'Leave it for now, Suzannah,' he said. 'Come and sit by me and let me tell you how beautiful you look.'

The bright blue of his eyes was as serious as she'd ever seen it as he asked, 'Dare I ask if you dressed for me?'

'Yes, of course I did,' she breathed. 'Every woman wants to be beautiful for the man in her life.'

'So you've definitely put that other guy, the one back in England, out of the running,' he said slowly.

Suzannah felt a shudder go through her. The answer to that was yes...yes...yes! She loathed Nigel. As far as she was concerned, he was out of her life for good, but was he going to leave it at that...and was she strong enough to face Lafe's disbelief if it came to a showdown?

'Yes. I've told you already,' she said quickly. 'I can't bear to even think of him.'

'So what was it that he did to make you hate him so?'

'I can't tell you. It hurts too much.'

'Then don't,' he said softly. 'His loss is my gain. For the last few years I feel as if I've been frozen, and not just because I've worked in a cold climate. My heart has been on ice. My plans have been the same. I've been living in some sort of suspended ice cube, but now, at last, I'm thawing out, and it's only happened since I met you.'

He had made no attempt to touch her as yet, and though

she longed for him to reach out for her, Suzannah was glad that the question she was about to ask would be before they came together.

Instinct was guiding her, along with a comment he'd once made that had stuck in her mind.

'Tell me what happened to your sister,' she said gently, 'because that's why you haven't been able to settle, isn't it?'

He turned slowly to face her and it was as if his light had gone out.

'Guilt is a terrible thing to live with, Suzannah,' he said flatly. 'Especially if it concerns one's nearest and dearest. It eats away at the soul. Takes away the joy of living...and is impossible to banish from the mind.'

Tell me about it, she thought bleakly as amazement washed over her. But what could this divine man have to feel guilty about?

She'd sensed his worth from the moment of their meeting and, whatever she was guilty of, there was no question in her mind as to whether Lafe Hilliard would have besmirched himself with some dark deed.

Taking his big capable hand in hers, she said softly, 'Are you going to tell me what happened?'

He sighed and it came from the depths of him. 'Nicolette and I were inseparable. She was two years younger but we were often taken for twins.

'You saw the house at St Anthony where we were brought up, didn't you? How the gardens run down to the beach?'

She nodded.

'We'd been to a party. She was a great girl for parties. I'd had plenty to drink while I was there. I'd even brought a bottle home with me. It was a very hot summer night, and while Nicolette was enjoying a midnight swim I lay on the grass, drinking the wine. That last bottle must have pushed me over the edge and while I was lying there in a drunken stupor she hit her head on a submerged rock and drowned.'

'Was there no one else around?' Suzannah asked gently.

Lafe shook his head. 'No. Our parents were on holiday. We had the house to ourselves. When I came round I staggered upstairs to bed, thinking that she'd already gone up before me. Her body was washed up on the beach the following morning.'

'But you can't blame yourself for that,' she exclaimed. 'You were foolish to have too much to drink, but thousands of people do that without any mishap. You weren't to know that your sister would hit her head...and drown.'

This is just too incredible for words, she was thinking. We're both carrying a burden of remorse, but Lafe's is one that he shouldn't have to shoulder. He has let grief become guilt, and that shouldn't have happened.

What happened to me is something completely different and there will always be someone, including myself, to remind me that I should have known better.

'Thank you for those kind words,' Lafe said with the beginning of a smile. 'I'll bear them in mind. Now, shall we get back to where we were? Me telling you that you're a beautiful woman.'

'Yes, please.' She sparkled back at him.

Lafe wasn't to know that she'd been living on a knife-edge since Nigel's appearance on the scene and that she had forebodings that tonight might be the grand finale to a friendship that she would treasure all her life.

As he swept her up in his arms it felt so right again. His mouth on hers was the promise of joy to come. His warm strength...bliss. His hands by their very touch telling her that they belonged...if only the fates would let it be so.

Let it last! she prayed as he laid her gently on his bed.

CHAPTER SIX

SUZANNAH had slept with Nigel once, and it had been a lustful, joyless experience which she'd been loth to repeat. It had marked the beginning of her disenchantment with him, and she'd thought since that it had perhaps been her reluctance for any further bedroom activities which had sparked off some of his spite.

It was so different with Lafe. There was a gentleness about his love-making that made her feel cherished. Yet there was fire in it, too. The fire that came from the loins of a man who lay with a beautiful woman.

As they each took their pleasure from the other, everything else was forgotten in the sublime moment of climax.

Afterwards, as Lafe lay sleeping with Suzannah in the warm circle of his arms, she began to wonder if this was the moment to tell him about her past. Maybe if he heard it from her own lips he wouldn't be so stunned.

Raising herself onto one elbow, she prepared to rouse him, but the moment was shattered as someone thudded on the cabin door and a voice called, 'Lafe! Come quickly! We have an emergency and we can't find Suzannah!'

His eyes flew open and he grimaced as the call was repeated.

'Ugh!' he groaned. 'It's only half past one. What's going on, I wonder?'

Suzannah was already standing beside the bed, replacing flimsy underwear with impressive speed. He gave a rueful smile. 'So much for our night of love, Dr Scott.'

Her heart twisted. She hoped that was how he saw it,

that he loved her as much as she loved him, but it wasn't the moment to pursue the matter.

'How am I going to get out of here without the rest of the staff seeing me?' she breathed.

Lafe was zipping up his jeans. 'Stay put until I'm gone and then make your departure. Yes?'

She nodded. 'Yes, and when I reappear I'll tell them that I've been taking a midnight stroll.'

He raised a disbelieving eyebrow. 'What, with three feet of snow as far as the eye can see?'

They both laughed, and with his hand on the doorhandle he said, 'Well, this is our life, here in Bramble Bay. Called out at all times of the day and night. I must be crazy. I turned down a consultant's job in St Anthony for this.'

'I'm coming!' he bellowed as voices could be heard again, and, bowing his head against the icy blast from outside, he went out into the night.

When Suzannah unobtrusively joined him some minutes later she was amazed to find Wayne Jones and his wife helping a heavily pregnant woman into the clinic. If her gasps of pain were anything to go by, she was about to give birth.

Her husband was by her side, white-faced and horrified, and Suzannah wondered what the woman was doing out here in the wilds in such a condition.

As they helped her onto the couch she gasped out the answer. 'We were trying to get to the hospital at Port aux Basques, but my pains, which were only mild when we set off, suddenly became severe.'

She took a deep breath and clung to the side of the bed as another contraction came. When it had gone she lay back, gasping, with beads of sweat on her forehead.

'Have you ever delivered a baby?' Lafe asked in a low voice after he'd examined her.

Suzannah shook her head. 'No. I was in paediatrics, not obstetrics. I suppose you have?'

He nodded. 'Yes, fortunately. Let's hope that it's a straightforward birth, though. We've no facilities here for anything else.'

'Where's Linda?' he asked of the unflappable Wayne.

'She went to the motel earlier. There was an Irish folk group on tonight.'

'And she's not back, I suppose?'

'It would appear not.'

'We can manage without her,' Suzannah said. 'She wasn't to know that this was going to happen...and she *is* off duty.'

'As we were,' he reminded her.

Not that she needed to be reminded. She was happier tonight than she'd been in months, and there was something in his smile that told her that Lafe was content, too.

He listened to the foetal heart rate during his examination of the pregnant woman, and as Suzannah looked at him questioningly he said, 'At the moment it's fine. Couldn't be better. A hundred and forty beats per minute.' With the grin that was essentially Lafe Hilliard on top of a situation, he said, 'At least we've got a foetal stethoscope.'

'We live in Port aux Basques,' the husband was explaining to Alison. 'My wife's mother hasn't been well and Candy wanted to manage one last visit before the baby came. But the labour pains started before we could get home. If you folks hadn't been here I don't know what we'd have done.'

He turned to Lafe. 'How far is she, Doctor?'

'Well on the way,' Lafe told him. 'The baby's heartbeat is strong and regular and it's not in a breach position or anything of a similar serious nature, so hopefully we might soon have some action.'

At that moment the woman cried out in agony as another

contraction gripped her. Lafe turned to Suzannah and said quickly, 'We're going to have to provide pain relief, and not having all the analgesics of a maternity unit to hand...'

She nodded. 'The lady says that it's a first baby, which makes one think it was a bit unwise to stray so far from home in the circumstances, but it's too late for worrying about that.'

'It certainly is,' he agreed in a low voice. 'As a primigravida we need a certain amount of dilatation—six centimetres at least—and contractions every two to three minutes before administering any kind of anaesthesia. I'm going to check her again and if we have that, then I think an injection into the epidural space is called for.'

He turned to the sombre male nurse. 'You're familiar with the procedure for dealing with the infant once it's been delivered, are you, Wayne?'

He shrugged. 'It's not something I've done before but there's always a first...and if Dr Scott will assist me?'

Suzannah smiled and her eyes were on the golden-haired figure beside him. 'I'd love to. This is turning out to be a night of new beginnings, isn't it?'

Wayne shook his head, not comprehending. 'If you say so.'

But Lafe's glance told her that he knew what she was on about and there was a warm promise in it that made her colour rise. Only an hour ago she'd been lying in his arms, sated and adrift with love for him...and now, in the middle of the night, they were about to deliver a child in the less than spacious confines of the Bramble Bay satellite clinic.

Within the hour they could see the baby's head, and as the young husband's face turned green Suzannah thought that there was going to be someone else needing her attention soon.

'Put his head between his knees,' she called over her shoulder to Alison, who was hovering anxiously as her husband checked that they had all the sterile equipment in position.

It wasn't a moment for squeamish husbands. Lafe was easing the baby outwards and as the mother gave one last painful cry it came and the man's expression changed from nausea to amazed wonder.

'You have a son,' Lafe told him.

'Has he got all his bits and pieces?' the man croaked.

'He has indeed,' Lafe replied.

The mother was watching the infant anxiously as so far it hadn't made a sound, but once Suzannah had wiped the mucus out of its mouth it gave a protesting wail.

When Lafe had clamped the cord and cut it, he laid the baby on his mother's stomach, telling her as he did so that in these first few seconds of life it needed the warmth of her body.

A goggle-eyed Linda had appeared at precisely the moment of birth and Maisie, of all people, had come across to see what was going on. She'd gone bustling into the kitchen and now they were all toasting the baby's health with mugs of hot tea. Altogether it was a moment of happy excitement for everyone except Suzannah.

It was an incredible experience to watch new life come into the world, but paradoxically it brought back the memory of a life that had been lost—just one of many in the history of a busy hospital, but it had been one that should have been saved and because of a tired young doctor and an arrogant consultant it had been put at risk.

'What is it, Suzannah?' Lafe asked when the baby had been cleaned up and placed in his mother's arms, wrapped in a soft white blanket. 'Didn't you think that was rather wonderful?'

'Yes, of course I did,' she choked. 'How could anyone think otherwise?'

'So what's wrong, then?'

She turned away. 'Nothing.'

'I don't believe you. It has to be something serious to make you look like that.'

'It was just a bad memory, Lafe, that's all. Don't mind me.'

He was smiling. 'But I do mind you. I mind everything about you. It's not so long ago that you lay in my arms in beautiful nakedness and that's something I won't forget in a hurry.'

'Neither will I,' she told him in a low voice, but the magic had gone. She was tainted, she thought wretchedly. Damned by her own hand.

Lafe thought that he had something to feel guilty about but it was as nothing compared to her transgression. Was she never going to be free of the pain of it? The scar had been healing and then what had happened? Nigel had arrived in Newfoundland and put her precarious peace of mind on a knife-edge. With that thought came another. How was he today? What length of time would it take for him to spoil her dream? For spoil it he would.

But the days went by and there was no word from Nigel. He'd been discharged from the hospital and where he'd gone she didn't know. She hoped it was back to England. But the hire car he'd been driving was still on view, a gleaming reminder of him on the forecourt of the clinic.

Maybe any day someone would call to return it to where it had come from, she told herself. There was no need for him to come personally. He could get an internal flight to St Johns and from there back to England. After all, he would be weak after the meningitis. The last thing he would feel like would be to come to Bramble Bay.

'Are you avoiding me by any chance?' Lafe asked after she'd made a pretence of being busy every time he wanted a word alone with her.

The answer was yes, but she wasn't going to tell him that. Easy and uncomplicated he might be, but those startling blue eyes didn't miss a thing, and if he got even an inkling of her state of mind Lafe wouldn't rest until she'd come into the open with whatever troubled her.

It would be so easy to do that. Spill it out to him. Get it out of her system. Confession was always a cleansing thing, but it was what would come afterwards that made her feel sick every time she thought about it.

'No. Of course I'm not,' Suzannah told him convincingly. 'It's just that I'm bogged down with folk suffering from winter ailments—influenza, falls on the ice, mild hypothermia, to name a few. Do you know that Maisie's neighbour, the old fellow who came in with the painful shoulder after chopping all that wood, has been sitting without heat in his house?'

'Why, for goodness' sake?' Lafe asked with a look in his eyes that said his mind was on her, rather than what she was saying.

'Because he's sold the wood, instead of keeping it for himself. Maisie reckons that he's not short of money, but he's an old skinflint. I've had to have serious words with him. Warning him of the dangers of letting one's body heat drop too low.'

Suzannah felt as if she was gabbling, but if it stopped Lafe from taking her in his arms, as his expression suggested he would very much like to, it was worth it. The closer they became, the more she dreaded losing him.

She had decided to go back to St Anthony to see John and his family during the coming weekend. She was missing them, and as their house was the only home she had at the present time she was looking forward to a couple of days of family life.

Her flat in Chester, back home in England, was being lived in by a friend until Suzannah decided to return, and any plans she might have had for finding herself a place in Newfoundland had been put on hold with the offer of the job in the clinic.

'Why the sudden decision?' Lafe asked with a new wariness born of her withdrawal from him.

'There's a Viking feast on Saturday night and John, Debbie and the children are going,' she told him. 'When I rang him on his birthday he asked why didn't I go with them. It's to be held in the big sod hut belonging to one of the restaurants, and I thought I'd take him up on the suggestion. It should be interesting, if nothing else.'

He was eyeing her thoughtfully. 'It's not a bad idea.'

'What? The Viking feast?'

'No. Going home for the weekend. We're both due some time off, and in any case we're supposed to be off duty at weekends. Although so far chance would have been a fine thing.

'In my case it would be a chance to call on the Realtor to discuss my house sale. I've heard nothing from them so far and have been too busy here to make enquiries. We'll take my Shogun, shall we? Then if any of the friendly neighbourhood moose come blundering out at us, I'll be in charge.'

With the feeling that she'd just been taken over, Suzannah nodded weakly. To be in Lafe's company would be a joy of the first order, but she was supposed to be keeping a low profile where Lafe was concerned. So much for that!

They hit the road early on Saturday morning, and as the Shogun lapped up the miles there wasn't even a glimmer of the moose population.

'It's later in the day that they appear,' Lafe said with a quick glance at the slender figure beside him.

In a warm, roll-necked sweater, jeans, and with heavy

boots on her feet, Suzannah was prepared for the weather that they might meet on the long journey to St Anthony, and Lafe was dressed likewise.

'What are you going to be wearing at the feast?' he asked when they stopped off for coffee at a roadside diner.

She laughed up at him, her worries put to one side in the pleasure of being there with him.

'A pair of long brown plaits, a leather tunic and open sandals.'

'I feel that I ought to be there to see that,' he joked, tuning into her mood. 'Do you think the organisers would have a spare ticket? I'm sure I could find something suitable to wear if I rummage through the wardrobes at home.'

'You don't need to dress up to look the part,' she said softly. 'From the day we met I've thought of you as a Viking, except for the fact that you're not rough and warlike, as they were.'

'Oh, no? It's plain to see that you've never seen me when I'm angry.'

Suzannah swallowed. 'Maybe one day the occasion will arise.'

His smile would have been totally reassuring if she hadn't felt so much like a prophet of doom. 'Not where you're concerned...my beautiful English doctor,' he told her teasingly.

'Don't!' she said sharply. 'Don't tempt providence, Lafe.'

'All right,' he agreed in mild surprise. 'Let's change the subject, shall we?'

And change it they did. But some of the magic had gone out of the morning and a couple of times she caught him eyeing her with a puzzled expression.

'Are you going to come in?' she asked of him some time later when they pulled up in front of John's house in St Anthony.

Lafe shook his head. 'No, thanks just the same. You'll have plenty to talk about with your family. I'll see you tonight at the feast.'

'So you think you'll be able to get a ticket?'

'Yes, I imagine so if I ask around. I've been to this sort of thing before and there are always spare ones available.'

''Zannah!' the boys cried when they saw Suzannah. 'How long have you come for?'

'Just the weekend,' she told them as she hugged them to her.

'Tell us what it's like, living on a satellite?' Richard cried. 'Do you have to wear spacesuits?'

'Er, no,' she said solemnly, avoiding his father's amused glance. 'The place where I'm working isn't up in the sky. It's just a clinic, like the ones where your mum takes you when you need to see the doctor or the dentist.'

'Oh, I see,' he said disappointedly. 'So you're not an astronaut?'

'Dumbo!' his brother exclaimed scornfully, and dragged him off to play.

'Any further sounds or sightings of the king rat?' John asked when the children had gone.

Suzannah shook her head. 'No. Nigel was discharged from hospital some days ago and I haven't a clue where he is. I'm hoping that he's gone back to England, but could I be so lucky?'

'What do you think Lafe will do if he finds out about what happened in England?'

'I don't know, John,' she said bleakly. 'I try not to think about it. I'm a good doctor and Lafe knows that, but I'm also a doctor who once made a dreadful mistake...and you know what they say about giving a dog a bad name.'

'You're in love with your gorgeous blond doctor, aren't you, Suzannah?' Debbie questioned gently.

'Yes, I am,' she confessed. 'Beside Lafe Hilliard, Nigel is lower than a snake in the grass.'

'Why not tell Lafe, then,' Debbie persisted, 'before the other fellow gets the chance to say anything catastrophic?'

'What? That I love him? Or about my murky past?'

'Both. One might soften the blow of the other.'

'I think Lafe knows that I love him,' she said wistfully, 'but ever since Nigel appeared on the scene he's finding my behaviour rather difficult to understand. He's going to join us at the Viking feast, by the way.'

'Whew! That will have heads turning,' Debbie teased. 'There won't be many women who don't clock Lafe Hilliard when he's out and about.'

The building in the grounds of a popular local restaurant was an authentic reproduction of the sod huts the Vikings had built for themselves when they'd landed at L'Anse aux Meadows, near Deerlake, a thousand years ago.

The inside was somewhat more modern, but the atmosphere of ancient culture had been maintained with animal skins on the floor, ancient implements scattered around and crude weapons fastened to the walls.

A group of amiable students greeted them as they went in. They were dressed appropriately for the occasion, as they were themselves, and as the atmosphere took hold Suzannah put her cares to one side and prepared to enjoy the evening.

Candles were the only form of illumination, and as a girl dressed as a slave offered them some sort of honey drink in stone goblets she looked around her.

There was no sign of Lafe as yet, but the place was full of Viking look-alikes and she thought that maybe he was here and she hadn't spotted him.

A group in the corner was making strange music on a selection of ancient-looking instruments, and the young master of ceremonies assured them laughingly that they would be able to dance to the peculiar refrain.

'Does he mean a war dance, do you think?' Debbie said as they found themselves a place at a rough wooden table.

'I don't know,' Suzannah said laughingly, 'but you can bet your life he's not referring to a waltz.'

At that moment her sister-in-law's prediction came true. Heads were turning and the reason was clear to see. Lafe Hilliard had just come striding in, putting all the other ancient warriors to shame.

He's magnificent, she thought with tender amusement as her glance took in the golden beard he'd found from somewhere and the strong tanned arms protruding from a leather tunic that hung above a pair of sturdy brown legs.

But it was the headpiece that was the master stroke. Two animal horns curved inwards above a metal helmet that sat upon his blond head as if it belonged there, and as he made his way to their table a cheer went up.

Unabashed, he bowed. Taking a crude blade from his waistband, he waved it around him in comic menace, to the delight of her young nephews.

'Greetings, wench,' he said as he lowered himself onto the rough plank that was the only seating provided, and with a bow for her companions added, 'And to the family Scott.'

'You look incredible,' Suzannah told him. 'Where did you find the gear?'

'I searched the attic. I have been to this kind of gathering before, you know...in my misspent youth maybe, but I do know the ropes.'

'You seem to know the ropes about everything.'

'Not everything,' he replied in a low voice. 'For instance, I don't know how to cope with a beautiful English doctor who's gone moody on me.'

There was an appeal in the hazel eyes meeting his. 'I'm

sorry if you think that, Lafe, because it isn't so. I've had something on my mind, yes, but I wouldn't want it to come between us.'

'So what is it?' he wanted to know.

Suzannah shook her head. 'It was nothing. It's past and forgotten.'

And if that wasn't wishful thinking, she didn't know what was! But time was passing and Nigel hadn't appeared, so maybe…

'So we can take up where we left off, then?' Lafe asked with a look that said he was prepared to do it there and then.

'When the time is right, yes,' she told him laughingly, 'but not with you wearing the beard…please.'

'If it's like the last time I held you in my arms I won't be wearing anything,' he teased.

If there was a reply to that she didn't get the chance to make it. It was time to partake of the feast. A young Viking was banging on a huge bronze gong and the buffet was declared open.

There was the ever-popular moose stew, a huge platter of the salt beef so popular with the Newfoundlanders and a succulent pig turning slowly on a spit.

Fresh fish dishes by the score were set out on a separate trestle, and as they carried their food back to the table Debbie whispered, 'Lafe loves you too, doesn't he, Suzannah?'

Suzannah's smile was rueful. 'Yes. I think he does. But Lafe is in love with the person he thinks I am. If he ever discovers the real me he might have a change of heart.'

'You spend too much time thinking about what happened back home,' her sister-in-law chided. 'It is the real you that he's seeing now. One mistake doesn't turn a caring young doctor into a monster.'

'Try telling that to the parents of a dead child,' she said wryly, and Debbie had no answer to that.

They'd eaten the food, drunk some strange but delicious drinks and danced to the Viking music. Now it was time to go. The boys were yawning, but protesting nevertheless, and as John and Debbie steered them purposefully towards the door Lafe said, 'Are you coming home with me, Suzannah?'

'Yes,' she said simply, as if it was the most natural thing in the world. But, then, it was. Lafe was like a magnet, drawing her to him with a force that she didn't want to escape.

As they drew up outside the house not long after that, it was just as memorable as before, gleaming whitely with the sea swishing choppily at the bottom of the garden.

But this time she was seeing the vast ocean in a different light. Its waters had taken Nicolette, the sister Lafe had adored, into their cold blue depths, and it was small wonder that he'd never settled there since.

Yet in spite of the tragedy all those years ago Suzannah was drawn to the old house. She could imagine herself living there with Lafe, loving him, caring for him, helping him to lay the ghosts that had turned him into a wanderer.

Her mouth twisted. She was the wrong one to be promising him that. She couldn't even cope with her own nightmares!

He'd seen her expression and as they stood side by side on the drive, with fleeces over their makeshift outfits to keep out the cold, he said quizzically, 'Welcome to the Hilliard homestead...again. Or have you changed your mind about coming in?'

'There's no likelihood of me changing my mind about that, or anything else,' she told him levelly.

'But you think that I might?' he threw back at her.

'Maybe.'

'Thanks for the vote of confidence.'

Suzannah shivered and it wasn't just because there was an icy wind.

'I'm cold. Can we go inside, please?'

'Yes, of course.'

After he'd unlocked the door Lafe stood back to let her pass, and as their bodies touched he pulled her to him and murmured, 'Don't shut me out again, Suzannah. Your thoughts were back in England again, weren't they?'

As she clung to him the temptation to come clean, to tell him her guilty secret, was so strong it brought tears to her eyes. Suddenly it seemed easy. For the sake of her peace of mind she was ready to risk everything. However, it was not to be confession time.

She'd heard voices coming from the water's edge further along when they'd got out of the car, but had taken little heed of them, except to think that it was a cold night to be beside the sea.

But now a shrill scream and panic-stricken shouting had them both frozen in alarm. As he removed his arms from around her Lafe said anxiously, 'That's the teenagers from next door. They're always larking about beside the water. Please, God, it's not history repeating itself!'

On that depressing note he began to run in the direction of the commotion. Suzannah was right behind him but he was outstripping her easily. She'd never seen anyone move so fast. Old terrors were giving wings to his feet.

There were three of them by the water's edge—a teenage girl and two boys. As she drew level Suzannah heard Lafe ask harshly, 'What's wrong?'

'It's Saskia,' the girl cried. 'We dared her to swim and she's disappeared.'

'Haven't I warned you about submerged rocks?' he roared as he wrenched off his jacket. 'And what kind of temperature do you think the water will be in this weather? The coldness of it could kill her. Is she in her right mind?'

Lafe didn't wait for an answer. He was already wading into the water, and as the group on the seashore watched he began to swim out with strong, urgent strokes.

In the light of a fitful moon the sea looked like a foaming black cauldron, and as she stood transfixed with horror Suzannah was praying that it wasn't going to be a repeat of what had happened all those years ago, but this time with two lives lost.

'He's got her!' one of the youths cried hoarsely. 'The Viking has got her!'

He had. Lafe was bringing the girl in, but they were still twenty feet from the shore.

Suzannah was tearing off her own topcoat, ready to go in to them if he got into difficulties, but, being the man he was, Lafe wasn't going to let another precious young girl go to a watery grave. As if the sea was ready to give up its victims, at that moment a huge wave came thundering behind them and swept them up onto the grassy bank.

As they pulled the limp figure of the girl away from the water's edge Lafe dragged himself alongside and then lay, gasping, on the grass beside her while Suzannah began to work on her frantically, with the youngsters crowding round.

For the first few moments there was no response, but she continued to resuscitate and suddenly a stream of water spurted from the girl's mouth and she began to moan weakly.

'Go and phone for an ambulance,' she told the boys. To the other girl she said, 'We've got to get her to the house and out of these wet clothes before she gets pneumonia or hypothermia or suchlike. We'll carry her between us.'

Lafe was struggling to his feet. 'I'll take her,' he said, and before Suzannah could protest he had picked the limp figure up in his arms and was hurrying across the sweeping lawns to the back entrance of the house.

CHAPTER SEVEN

AFTER the paramedics had taken charge of the bedraggled Saskia, and the ambulance had gone speeding towards the hospital, Lafe and Suzannah went back to his house.

He was still in the sodden Viking outfit, and before he went for a hot bath he said wryly, 'Not much of a fine figure at the moment, am I?'

'You were incredible out there,' she told him softly. 'It was so dark and the sea was so rough. I thought you were both going to be drowned. They were some of the worst moments of my life.'

'There was no way I was going to let it happen all over again,' he said grimly. 'It was as if the fates were giving me a second chance, and I wasn't going to bungle it.'

'I understand that, but you were battling against the elements out there in very dangerous waters. It was terrifying!'

'Hmm, I suppose it was,' he agreed, 'but there was no time to worry about that. I had to get her out.'

He looked down at the puddle that his wet clothes were making on the kitchen floor. 'As soon as I've made myself presentable I want to go to the hospital to see how she is. I don't know where the parents are but they'll go crazy when they hear about this.'

'One of the boys, the one I presume to be her brother, said they'd gone to St Johns on business and aren't due back until tomorrow,' Suzannah informed him.

'All the more reason for me to be there, then,' he remarked as he squelched towards the stairs.

She nodded. 'I'll go with you.'

If it had occurred to Lafe that they were spending the night in very different circumstances to what they'd planned, he didn't comment.

He just touched her cheek with a cold, wet hand and said, 'Fine. I won't be long.'

Saskia was fully conscious when they got to the hospital, and as they approached the bed she gave a shamefaced smile.

'I'm sorry, Dr Hilliard,' she told him contritely. 'I was an idiot. The others dared me to have a late night swim and I took them up on it.'

'Haven't I told you how dangerous this part of the coast is?' he said tersely.

She hung her head. 'Yes.'

'I hadn't mentioned it before as I didn't want to alarm you, but maybe I should have. My sister was drowned in that very spot many years ago. She hit her head on a submerged rock and never surfaced again.'

'You could have succumbed to the same fate…or been overcome by the coldness of the water,' Suzannah said gently. 'It was lucky for you that Dr Hilliard heard your cries.'

She knew that the girl was contrite but she could have shaken her for what she'd done. Both Saskia and Lafe could have been drowned if it hadn't been for his strength and determination.

The hospital had checked him over and pronounced him all right, no doubt because he'd been in the water for less time than Saskia.

'I want to go home,' the crestfallen Saskia was saying, 'but the doctor says they're going to keep me in for observation.'

'That's a necessary precaution,' Lafe said, feeling for the

limp hand on the coverlet. 'Your body heat seems to be getting back to normal.'

'It is now,' she agreed, 'but they had to wrap me in foil in the ambulance. I was so cold I thought I'd died.'

'So you're not going to do anything like that again?'

Saskia shuddered. 'No way!'

It was half past three when they left the hospital and, instead of driving back to his place, Lafe turned in the direction of John's house.

When she eyed him questioningly he gave a wry smile. 'I'm not fit company for you tonight, Suzannah...for what's left of it anyway. I'm shattered after that episode and feeling less than lively.'

'Yes, of course,' she told him with a quick glance at his downcast face, 'but before we part there's something I want to say.'

His head came up at that. 'Don't put any more weight on my shoulders.'

'I'm not going to. I just want to point out, in case you haven't thought of it already, that tonight you've redeemed yourself. Some strange quirk of fate allowed you to do what you couldn't do for Nicolette all that time ago. You've balanced the scales. Be thankful. Let tonight's trauma be a cleansing thing, because I'm sure that's what your sister would want.'

He sighed. 'I suppose you're right, my wise one. But at the moment I'm not thinking straight at all. Maybe tomorrow I will.

'Kiss me, Suzannah,' he said as they stopped outside John's house.

'That's an invitation I can't refuse,' she teased gently, but it was a butterfly kiss on the cheek that she gave him. If ever there was a moment when passion was the last thing in their minds, this was it.

As Suzannah went quietly up to her room in the silent

house, Lafe's words, when she'd said she had something to say, came back to mind. 'Don't put any more weight on my shoulders,' he'd said.

At that moment he'd been at his lowest ebb. The fact that he'd saved young Saskia's life wasn't creating any euphoria in him. His thoughts had been on that other time long ago when, due to nothing other than youthful stupidity, he'd failed his sister. But surely after this, when he'd spent some time in rational thought, he would feel better.

The northern lights were out, beautiful beyond belief, but tonight Suzannah was barely aware of them. His plea that she bring him no further burdens to carry was still haunting her as she fought to decide which Lafe would see as the worst, were he ever to come to hear of it—her deceit, or her unforgivable negligence.

When Suzannah appeared for breakfast the next morning Debbie raised surprised eyebrows. 'I thought you were...er...out,' she said.

'I was, but Lafe's teenage neighbours put paid to that.'

'In what way?'

'The girl went into the sea on a dare and got into difficulties.'

John's glance lifted from the book he was reading. 'On a night like that! Crazy young madam!'

'And?' Debbie asked in concern.

'Lafe went in and brought her out.'

It sounded so simple, put like that. There was no hint of the terror that had gripped her in the bald statement, but Debbie understood.

'My nerves!' she exclaimed. 'He could have been drowned like his poor sister.'

'Yes, I know,' Suzannah agreed, 'and the girl, too.'

'And so where are they now?' John wanted to know.

'Lafe went home to recharge his batteries and the girl

has been kept in hospital for observation. He's picking me up later.'

'It's a strange thing,' she said to Debbie after John and the boys had left to go skating on a nearby lake, 'but every time I'm about to come clean to Lafe something prevents me. I was going to tell him last night, but before I could do so we were involved in the rescue and after that, well...'

'If he's meant to know, he'll find out,' Debbie pointed out philosophically. 'But you can't marry the man with something like that on your mind. You owe it to him, 'Zannah. He's a lovely guy.'

'Yes, he is,' she agreed softly. 'When I compare him to that wretch Nigel Summers, I can't believe how stupid I was. I suppose I was flattered that one of the top consultants at the hospital was interested in me and it prevented me from seeing straight....but who says Lafe is going to ask me to marry him?'

'I do,' her sister-in-law said laughingly. 'He's got to. I've never been a maid-of-honour.'

Lafe was back to his usual equable self when he called for her later that morning, and Suzannah breathed a sigh of relief. He'd been unusually downcast the night before and not without reason. Hopefully, the painful memories the incident had evoked were receding.

'I do feel better about Nicolette,' he said as the Shogun pulled out onto the road that would take them back to Bramble Bay. 'You were right in what you said last night, Suzannah. Saving young Saskia doesn't make my sorrow any less, but I do feel that I've atoned in part.'

She smiled, the warmth of her love for him in the bright hazel gaze meeting his.

'Good,' she told him. 'The only way for you now is forward. Put down some roots...and I don't mean in

Bramble Bay. We're doing a good service there but it's time you were employed according to your potential.'

'I'll bear all that in mind,' he said with mock earnestness, and they both began to laugh.

If Suzannah's mirth wasn't as easily come by as his, he didn't notice. But she knew that she was the last one to be telling him how to live his life.

Tired after their interrupted night, she fell asleep on the long ride back, and as she lay curled up in the seat beside him Lafe pulled to the side of the road.

Taking a rug from the back of the car, he wrapped it around her and then sat looking down at her, his face sombre in the fading light of the winter afternoon.

She was beautiful and clever, he thought. The gods must have been smiling down on him that day up on the hill behind Grenfell's house. But there was something in her manner that puzzled him.

He was pretty sure that she was attracted to him...that she enjoyed being with him...and that she was happy working with him at the clinic. But what was it she'd said? It was time for him to be looking forward? Putting down roots?

That had been the gist of it. But there'd been no mention that she would like to be part of it. That she saw a future for them...together. It was as if Suzannah had been dissociating herself from what she was saying.

There was something about her that he couldn't fathom. Was he going to have to wait until she enlightened him, or what? He'd waited a long time for this to happen and wished he didn't feel so uneasy.

They were slithering to a halt on freshly fallen snow in front of her cabin when Suzannah opened her eyes.

'Oh, no!' she groaned. 'Don't tell me I've been asleep all the way.'

''Fraid so. Didn't you want to be?'

'No! I didn't,' she told him, feeling irritable that she'd wasted all the hours that they'd been together. 'You must have found me totally boring.'

'No, I didn't. I haven't forgotten that you had very little sleep last night.'

'The same applies to you.'

'I'm used to it.'

He was smiling across at her. 'We got seriously sidetracked, didn't we, Suzannah?'

'Mmm,' she murmured, still drowsy.

'So when are we going to make up for it?'

Before she could come up with an answer to that, Linda appeared at the side of the car, and when Suzannah heard what she had to say the necessity for a reply was no longer there.

'There's a guy waiting to see you,' the nurse informed her. 'He's been camped out in the waiting room at the clinic since this morning.'

'Does he have a name?' Suzannah said slowly.

'Yes. But you'll probably know him better as the fellow that the hunting party brought here, suffering from meningitis.' And with that she hugged her jacket around her and dashed back inside.

'I think that Dr Scott knows me for more personal reasons than that, eh, Suzannah?' Nigel's voice chipped in suddenly from the other side of the car. 'We've worked together and were once engaged to be married.'

'What are you doing here, Nigel?' she cried angrily. 'I told you that day at Port aux Basques that I want nothing more to do with you.'

'So how about making yourself scarce,' Lafe said coldly.

'Ah, I see. So it's like that, is it?' Nigel sneered. 'You've found yourself another medic, Suzannah. You're combining work with pleasure again.'

Lafe was out of the car and moving purposefully towards

him. 'Suzannah has told me about you and she wants nothing more to do with you,' he snapped. 'So you'd better be on your way...friend.'

Nigel's eyes were glittering. She knew what was coming next. He'd been only too quick to steer clear of her when she'd been in trouble, but for some perverted reason he now wanted her back, and the fact that he'd guessed there was something between Lafe and herself would make him all the more peevish.

'So she's been confiding in you, has she? How touching. I'll bet she didn't tell you that back home it was her negligence that caused a child to die and that's why she's rooting around in the backwoods.'

Suzannah saw Lafe freeze in mid-stride, but whatever he was thinking he wasn't going to give the other man the satisfaction of seeing him taken aback.

'I don't allow the conduct of my staff to be discussed in public, or anywhere else for that matter,' he gritted. 'So if you've said what you came to say, get in that damned car of yours that we're sick of the sight of and clear off. If I see you anywhere near this place again you'll live to regret it.'

'I have contacts in England who could make life very difficult for you both,' Nigel cried as he backed away.

'Making life difficult for others seems to be your forte,' Lafe said in steely tones. 'I'll give you five minutes to be on your way.'

'I'm going!' Nigel snarled. 'But I wouldn't let her loose on your patients if I were you.'

As he drove off in the hire car with a defiant screech of tyres Lafe said flatly, 'You'd better come into my cabin, Suzannah. We're less likely to be disturbed there than at your place.'

'Sit down,' he said heavily when they'd taken off their topcoats.

When she'd obeyed he stood looking down at her as if he were seeing her for the first time, and all her forebodings came back a thousandfold.

'So, Suzannah?' he said in a voice that was so unlike his usual tones that she wanted to run away and hide. 'I could tell there was a lot of venom coming from that guy, but there's rarely smoke without fire.'

She nodded mutely and he went on, 'During recent weeks I've sensed that you've had something on your mind, but whenever I've asked you about it you've fobbed me off. Now I realise that you became worse about the time that they brought this Summers fellow in with meningitis.

'In the light of what has just happened it would appear that you recognised him, but for some reason best known to yourself you didn't say so. Which makes me think that visiting him at Port aux Basques wasn't the sort of thing you would do for just any patient. Am I right?'

'Yes. You're right,' she admitted dismally.

'I must have been very stupid to let myself be taken in by your clever little charade.'

'It wasn't meant to be like that!' she protested desperately. 'As soon as I saw Nigel on the day when the hunting party brought him here I knew it had something to do with me, but I didn't know what. We'd parted on the very worst of terms. I detest him totally.'

'So why did he come here, then?'

'He wants me back.'

'I see. So we've clarified that part of your deceit, but from what I've gathered during that unpleasant confrontation there could be more to come.'

When she didn't answer he said, 'Are you going to tell me about what happened, then?'

'A child in my care died. She was taken off steroids without any gradual phasing off...and it was fatal.'

The eyes meeting hers were colder than a Newfoundland winter.

'Any doctor knows the danger of doing that!' he said with chilly incredulity.

She opened her mouth to tell him what had happened. That she would always feel guilty for letting herself be despatched from the ward, but it had been Nigel, her superior, who had given the order for the drug to be withdrawn.

But what was the point? Even if Lafe ended up sympathising with her, which in light of his cold anger was most unlikely, he would still see her as devious and deceitful.

On the day the hunters had brought Nigel in, she'd let Lafe treat the sick man without admitting that he was known to her. That must seem incredible to him, and then, only seconds ago, he'd had to listen to Nigel's vile accusations.

It was her own fault. She shouldn't have let herself be sidetracked those other times when she'd wanted to open her heart to the man she loved, and now it was too late.

She'd hesitated because she'd been so desperate to find a purpose in life. So attracted by the clean, uncomplicated charm of Lafe that she hadn't wanted to risk it.

'You've deceived me twice,' he was saying. 'By not telling me about what happened in England and by concealing the fact that you knew the Summers guy. How come the hospital authorities back there recommended you?'

'I was cleared at the hearing because I'd done nothing wrong,' she whispered. 'Any deception on my part has been because I'm weighed down with guilt. I let Nigel do something I knew was wrong, and I've been paying the price ever since.'

'And so who ended the engagement?' he asked, as if she hadn't spoken.

'I did.'

Tell him, a voice inside her was saying. Now is your chance to vindicate yourself. Lafe has seen for himself what Nigel's like. Explain what he did to you.

But pride was rearing its head. Whatever Nigel had done, she had been the one who'd let him get away with it. Nothing was ever going to change that. Let Lafe judge her on what he already knew.

'What are you going to do?' she asked dully.

'With regard to what?'

'Us? The job?'

'Your work, since I took you on, has been faultless, and with the backing of your hospital manager in England I see no reason to change anything in that respect. But needless to say, Suzannah, I shall be watching you. You've shown yourself to be secretive and untrustworthy. Characteristics that do not appeal to me. Which brings me to your other question. What about us?'

Lafe's voice was completely devoid of any kind of emotion as he went on, 'I think you know the answer to that already...and I'd like you to go now. I have some thinking to do.'

'Did you get any sleep last night?' Shirley asked when Suzannah appeared the next morning. 'I heard you prowling around like a caged animal.'

'Er...no...not a lot,' she admitted. 'I was restless for some reason.' If that wasn't the understatement of all time, she didn't know what was!

'There was that guy waiting for you,' Shirley went on. 'The English fellow. Did you see him?'

'Yes. I saw him,' she said listlessly. She'd seen and heard him, and life would never be the same again.

Involved in getting her breakfast and preparing for a day with the aches and pains of whoever needed her services,

Shirley didn't pursue the matter, to Suzannah's relief and once the physiotherapist had gone bustling across to the clinic Suzannah followed at a slower pace.

For the first time since they'd met she wasn't eager to see Lafe. Would he have changed his mind since the previous night? she wondered. And if he had, would it be for the better...or worse?

When they came face to face in the surgery she saw that nothing had changed. He was coldly polite, spoke merely about the duties of the day ahead, and only seemed to perk up when Linda came breezing in with her own brand of brash charm.

At that moment Suzannah had little to be thankful about, but one thing she was grateful for. The pushy nurse hadn't been there when Nigel had done his demolition job.

Monday morning almost always brought a full waiting room and today was no different. They usually shared the patients between them, but on this occasion Lafe had other ideas.

'I'm going to Port aux Basques,' he said abruptly. 'I should be back some time late this afternoon.'

Her heart began to thud. 'So are you going to recommend to the authorities that I should lose my job for being untrustworthy?'

His mouth was a straight, uncompromising line as he eyed her from across the room. 'Did I say that?'

'You don't have to. It's all I can expect. I don't blame you.'

He sighed. 'If you must know, I'm going to meet a friend of mine who's coming over on the ferry from Nova Scotia and is staying in the town for a while.'

'Oh, I see,' she said lamely, wishing she'd kept quiet. Then on a sudden angry impulse she added, 'So you're trusting me to take surgery on my own? You're not afraid that the patients might be at risk?'

'Why? Are they?'

She shook her head. 'Of course not!'

'Then hadn't you better get on with it? If you keep them waiting any longer they'll be giving you the slow handclap.'

As the morning progressed there was no time to brood on the collapse of her relationship with Lafe. No sooner had she seen to one patient than another was facing her on the other side of the desk.

Michael Ericson was one that lingered in the mind. Manager of a lumber yard a short way along the coast, he looked as fresh and clean as the fish that a previous patient had given her from his catch.

'So what's the problem?' Suzannah asked as a pair of wary grey eyes met hers.

'I've got a lump in a very awkward place,' he said.

'And where might that be?' she asked in her most businesslike manner.

'In my testicle.'

'I see. I'd better have a look at it, then. Or would you prefer to wait until Dr Hilliard is on duty?'

'Er...no. We're busy at the lumber yard. I don't know when I'll be able to get here again.'

'Fine. Then take off your trousers, please.'

She'd known male patients who would endure any amount of pain rather than do that, but even though she sensed that he was embarrassed Michael Ericson was prepared to do as she asked. As for herself, she was so deep in the depths of misery that if she'd suddenly found a huge moose in the chair opposite, it would have made no impact.

'I'm almost sure that it's a benign cyst,' she told him when she'd finished examining him, 'but I'm not going to take any chances. We'll have a scan and X-rays done just to make sure that it's not malignant.'

He swallowed hard. 'So there's a possibility that it might be cancer?'

'Yes,' she told him levelly. 'There's always a chance of that when lumps appear out of the blue. But in your case I'm pretty sure that it's a cyst.'

After he'd put his trousers back on he said, 'Thanks, Doctor. I'm much obliged.'

She nodded. 'The hospital will be in touch with an appointment, Mr Ericson.'

A very old lady with a bent back followed him, and as Suzannah got up to help her to the chair she said in a surprisingly strong voice, 'I'm Alice Cabot. I've never seen a doctor before, but my sons say I've no excuse now that we have a clinic on our doorstep.'

Suzannah smiled into the old nutmeg face. 'That's what we're here for, Mrs Cabot. For those who can't travel to Port aux Basques for any reason or those who aren't sick enough to need hospital treatment—and for emergencies. The main hospital has to cover a huge area and it's clinics like this that help to ease the burden. So, would you like to tell me what the problem is?'

'Age,' the old woman replied. 'I'm a hundred and two years old and looking after my sons isn't as easy as it was.'

'Your sons?' Suzannah echoed. They had to be pensioners themselves, she thought.

'Yes. They're fishermen. We've been fishing folk all our lives.'

'You'll remember Wilfred Grenfell, then?'

Her face lit up. 'The doctor! Of course I do. My father used to talk about him. Many was the time he travelled over the ice to attend him as my daddy had something wrong with his lungs. There could be a blizzard raging, with the wind like a knife, and there'd be his sledge slithering to a stop outside the house. He would have icicles on his moustache and his dogs would be puffing and panting after the journey, but if he heard that he was needed, the doctor was there.

'He always stayed for a cup of strong black tea. We couldn't afford milk and sugar in those days. Then before he went he'd say a prayer and read a few verses from the Bible.'

'I come from the same English town as Wilfred Grenfell,' Suzannah told the woman.

'My nerves!' Alice exclaimed. 'Would you believe it? You're doctoring in the same places that he did!'

'Yes, I am,' she agreed with a wan smile.

She was...for the present. But it was only by the skin of her teeth. Even if Lafe didn't decide to dispense with her services, she might end up feeling that she couldn't stick it any longer.

'And so what are we going to do about you?' she said gently, bringing her mind back to her patient's needs.

'When I was young we found nearly all our cures in the woods,' the old woman said, 'but there wasn't ever anything to make us young again. Could you suggest some medicine I could take to give me my strength back, Doctor? Or have I got an appointment with St Peter?'

'I'm going to examine you first,' Suzannah told her. 'I want to check your heart and lungs. You're not wearing glasses so I presume that your eyes are all right?'

'I can see when I'm outside but I need 'em for reading.'

When she'd finished, Suzannah was smiling. 'You're in remarkably good shape for your age, Mrs Cabot. I think a course of vitamins and some help around the house is what you need.'

'So I'm not going to leave my lads yet?'

'No, not yet, as far as I can see. But don't your sons have wives to care for them?'

She laughed, showing a mouth full of yellow teeth. 'No. Four of 'em and not one of 'em married.'

'So you have no grandchildren to bring joy to your old age?'

Alice chuckled. 'I said as how they weren't married, Doctor. I didn't say I had no grandchildren. When my lads were in their prime, they had the pick of all the women, but never wanted to settle down. Fifteen grandchildren at the last count, and they've all got children who've got young 'uns of their own, too…'

Smiling as Alice began to give her a detailed account of her extremely large family, Suzannah pulled the prescription pad towards her and began to write.

As the day wore on the weather began to worsen. Gale-force winds ripped around the clinic, bringing with them icy sleet that chilled to the bone.

A fishing boat owned by a man further along the shore had arrived back after a severe battering, to the relief of all concerned. And a truck loaded with logs from the lumber yard where Michael Ericson ruled the roost had stopped nearby because the force of the wind was shifting its load.

Had Lafe seen the weather and decided to stay in Port aux Basques for the night? Suzannah wondered. Or was he on his way back in these dreadful conditions? She hoped not.

The fact that he'd let her see how disenchanted he was with her, and had withdrawn from any contact other than the job, didn't make him any less precious in her sight.

It was only a couple of nights since she'd been terrified that he might drown. Now she was agonising over his safety in some of the worst weather she'd seen since arriving in Newfoundland.

Maybe the phone would ring at any second to say that he'd stayed put, she told herself as darkness fell. Disgusted with her he might be, but Lafe would be concerned about the running of the clinic in his absence. Especially as he'd lost confidence in her.

But as the winter's night closed in there was no message, and there was nowhere that she could ring him as she didn't know where he was. The friend arriving from Nova Scotia was something he'd flung at her out of the blue. Which meant that either he'd forgotten to mention it earlier, or he'd had a phone call the previous evening.

At eleven o'clock there had still been no word from him and she undressed and put on a warm robe.

'What's wrong?' Shirley asked. 'You're on edge. I can tell.'

'I'm wondering if Lafe is all right,' Suzannah said uneasily.

'Why, where is he? I thought I hadn't seen him around the place.'

'He went off earlier in the day to meet the ferry at Port aux Basques and I've heard nothing from him since. And in this weather…'

'You're not going to wait up, are you?' Shirley asked. 'If I remember rightly, you were awake most of last night. You must be dropping in your tracks.'

'I'll hang on for a while,' Suzannah said. 'He might ring in, needing help.'

Shirley laughed. 'Wanting us to arrive with shovels to dig him out, you mean?'

'Something like that,' she agreed, as the thought of him freezing and lost, somewhere out in the wilds, made her own blood run cold.

CHAPTER EIGHT

IT WAS two o'clock in the morning when Suzannah heard the Shogun pull up outside the cabins. She was lying on top of the bedcovers in the darkness, her ears straining for the sound of an engine, her mind crowded with apprehensive thoughts and sleep a thousand miles away in spite of it being her third night of broken sleep.

When she heard the crunch of tyres outside she was on her feet in an instant, relief washing over her in a gladsome tide. Lafe was back, thank God! He was safe! Somehow he'd managed to surmount the awful weather conditions and return to the fold.

She hurried to the window and pulled back the curtain in time to see him walking slowly towards his cabin with a weary droop to his broad shoulders. Whether from exhaustion after what must have been a nightmare journey, or from the disillusion for which she was responsible, she wasn't sure, but whatever the cause her heart ached for him.

It took all her control not to rush outside and hold him close, but the old intimacy had gone and if he knew she'd waited up until this hour he would think she was crazy.

With his hand on the doorhandle Lafe turned and looked across to where she was standing half-hidden by the curtain. She moved back, praying that he hadn't spotted her. It would be too embarrassing if he'd seen her spying on him.

It seemed that he hadn't as he was pushing the door back and disappearing into his own sanctum, so with her vigil now over Suzannah threw off her robe and climbed between the sheets.

* * *

As Lafe threw himself wearily into a chair beside the stove that burned day and night to heat the cabin he was wishing that Suzannah had been waiting for him.

In spite of the hour, it would have been heaven to be held close in the moment of return, to breathe in her perfume and feel her smooth skin next to his, but it was impossible.

He was a tolerant, reasonable sort of man, but he didn't like being made to look a fool and the elegant English doctor had done just that.

What she'd said she'd done back home in England had been human error and he could forgive her that. She had also been cleared. But why in the name of glory hadn't she told him?

He didn't flatter himself that it had been because she'd been desperate to work for him. They'd hardly known each other at that time, but there had to be some sort of reason why she'd kept quiet.

Maybe it was to do with the unpleasant Nigel Summers, but if it was, she wasn't prepared to come clean about that either. Every time he thought about it he felt sick and he knew that Suzannah was miserable, too, but she had only herself to blame for that.

He'd enjoyed today's meeting with a colleague he'd worked with in the Arctic, but he thought guiltily that he must have seemed less than interested with his mind on Suzannah all the time.

Then, like someone with a death wish, he'd set off back in deplorable weather, an action that he would have condemned in anyone else. He supposed he was lucky to be back in one piece.

As he sat gazing into the glowing coals inside the stove her words came back to him. She'd told him it was time to go forward—to put down roots. What a joke!

* * *

Suzannah surfaced the next morning to hear Shirley enquiring if she was intending to take the day off as it was only fifteen minutes to clinic time.

'Wha-at?' she groaned, swinging herself slowly out of the bed. 'I don't believe it!'

'You have to, I'm afraid,' she was told. 'I see that Lafe got back safely. What time did you come to bed?'

'Shortly after you,' she fibbed.

'And some!' Shirley said in amused disbelief.

'Well, maybe it was a bit later than that.'

The accommodating physiotherapist put a cup of tea in her hand. 'You've time to drink that. I can't see Lafe being up with the lark this morning.'

But of course he was. Just to be awkward, Suzannah thought when she presented herself a short time later and found him already at his desk, taking a phone call.

When she hesitated in the doorway he beckoned her forward and, after replacing the receiver, eyed her thoughtfully for a moment. 'That was the airport at St Johns. They've just confirmed that passenger Nigel Summers flew out on a Heathrow flight early this morning.'

Suzannah let out a sigh of relief but his expression hadn't altered. 'I spoke to him at his hotel before he left and—'

'How did you know where he was staying?' she asked in sick surprise.

'The hospital at Port aux Basques gave me the information. They'd asked him where he was going to be based, so that they could forward him the details of the treatment he'd received here. The authorities in the UK will want to know about it, meningitis being the contagious thing that it is.'

'And what did you say to him?' Suzannah asked weakly.

'Just words to the effect that he had better be on that plane.'

'He could still try to make things difficult here when he gets back in England,' she pointed out.

'We'll cross that barrier when and if we get to it,' Lafe said dismissively. 'I just called you in to let you know that Summers has gone.'

'Yes. I see. Thanks for taking the trouble,' she said quietly. Then, on an impulse that she couldn't ignore, she went on, 'Did you have trouble getting back last night?'

'Why do you ask?'

As if he didn't know that everything about him was her concern!

'I thought I heard you drive up some time during the night.'

'Yes. I had to dig the car out a couple of times. But I was also late in leaving Port aux Basques.'

'Did your friend arrive all right?'

Suzannah was being nosy but couldn't help it. The longing to be back to the way they had been was overpowering, but the chances weren't looking good.

'Serena? Yes, she arrived on time. We had a very nice day, catching up with each other's news.'

Suzannah was goggling at him. Why had she taken it for granted that it had been a man friend that he'd gone to meet?

'What?' he questioned abruptly, on seeing her expression.

'Er...nothing.'

'She was one of the scientists at Ice Station Mercury for a short time.'

'I see.'

'Hmmm. I'm sure that you do...and now, if you'll excuse me, I need to have a word with Linda. While I'm doing that perhaps you'll see what the waiting-room situation is like.'

'Yes, of course.'

She'd been dismissed. Politely, and of necessity, but dismissed nevertheless. They could have been strangers for all the warmth there'd been in his voice.

'I've been having shocking headaches,' Suzannah's first patient told her.

He was a middle-aged man with the stamp of the outdoors upon him, and when she asked what his occupation was, it was easy to see why.

'I'm a game warden,' he said, 'out in all weathers. Usually I don't ail a thing, but these headaches are really bad.'

His blood pressure was high but not dangerously so, and the man reckoned that he'd had his eyes tested not so long ago, which left the possibility of a stress-related problem or something more sinister.

It transpired that he'd recently gone through an acrimonious divorce and was having difficulty seeing his children, which might have been reason for stress, but, taking no chances, she referred him to the main hospital for a brain scan.

The owner of a small home for the elderly further along the coast had asked for a call to one of her patients, and once she'd dealt with those waiting to be seen Suzannah prepared to set off.

Weather conditions were still bad but the wind had dropped and gritting had been carried out on the main highway that ran past the clinic. With luck it should be a short, safe drive.

As she went to put on her outdoor clothes she saw that Shirley was attending to a fisherman who'd had a badly fractured wrist, the two nurses were occupied with various minor matters and Alison, with her usual quiet efficiency, was dealing with a new arrival at the reception desk.

'This lady is asking for Dr Hilliard,' she said when Suzannah appeared. 'Is he free, do you know?'

She could have told Alison that the man in question had

never been more free if the state of their relationship was anything to go by, but the strange woman was swivelling round to face her.

'I'm Serena Bradley, a friend of Dr Hilliard's,' she said with a charming smile. 'I believe he's expecting me.'

Suzannah swallowed hard. This Arctic scientist was a very attractive woman. As fair-skinned as Lafe himself, but petite with it, she looked more fitted to life in a beauty salon than amongst the frozen wastes. And she'd turned up at just the right time to offer consolation, should Lafe be seeking it, after her own fall from grace.

As they shook hands Suzannah said, 'Lafe is around somewhere. If you'd like to come with me, I'll seek him out for you.'

They found him beside the Shogun, chatting to the mechanic who'd rescued her Jeep after the moose incident on their first journey to Bramble Bay, and as she watched his face light up at the sight of her companion Suzannah had never felt more insignificant.

'Serena!' he said warmly. 'So you've made it. I tried to phone you this morning to tell you not to come over today. The weather I travelled home in last night was foul, but it improved quite quickly, so I guessed that you must have already set off.

'There's something wrong with my car,' he said to Suzannah in less welcoming tones. 'It's going to have to go into the garage. If we're called out we'll have to use yours.'

'Obviously,' she agreed drily, on the point of departing from an encounter where she was surplus to requirements.

'You can use *my* car if need be,' the new arrival volunteered. 'But first you're going to show me around the clinic, aren't you, Lafe?'

There was a smile on his face but Suzannah saw that it wasn't beaming in her direction. Keeping to her previous intention, she turned to go, saying over her shoulder, 'I've been called to the home for the elderly.'

To the likeable visitor she said pleasantly, 'Nice to have met you, Serena.'

With that she went, wishing as she did so that Serena Bradley hadn't turned out to be such an attractive diversion.

What was she doing in Newfoundland, anyway? she thought irritably as she eased the Jeep carefully onto the icy road. Was she just passing through the area and had decided to look Lafe up? Or was it a previous arrangement that they'd made?

Whatever it was, it was none of her business...now.

Myrtle Stephens wasn't as old as the active centenarian Alice Cabot and neither was she as well. The seventy-six-year-old had been in the nursing home for some time with severe bronchial problems and failing eyesight due to diabetes.

When Suzannah went up to see her in a neat bedroom overlooking the sea she found the elderly lady very poorly.

'The lungs are affected,' she told the sister in charge after she'd examined her. 'Mrs Stephens has got pneumonia. She needs hospital care. I'm going to ask for her to be admitted as soon as possible.'

'Yes. I understand,' the sister said soberly, 'but Myrtle is almost blind. It will be very frightening for her to be moved from this place where she can just about find her way around.'

Suzannah nodded. 'I realise that, but I have no choice but to send her to hospital. I can ask that once she's over the worst she be sent back here as soon as possible, but she has to go, I'm afraid.'

'Unless I die,' Myrtle wheezed, and looking at Suzannah with watery eyes. 'Am I likely to?'

'Not if I can help it, Mrs Stephens,' Suzannah replied cheerfully.

'Well, we'd better get going, then,' the old lady said. 'Are you going to pack my bag, Sister? You can tell the rest of the folks in here that I'll be coming back to plague them.'

Suzannah patted her hand. 'That's the right attitude, Mrs Stephens. You hang on in there and I'll go to phone for an ambulance.'

They were tough, these old Newfoundlanders, Suzannah thought as she drove back to the clinic. But how had they coped before it had been there? The best they could, she supposed. And how many had died in the past because the source of care was so far away?

It was lunchtime when she got back and there was no sign of Lafe and his visitor. The rest of the staff were sitting around, eating a quick sandwich, and as if reading her mind Linda said pertly, 'If you're looking for our leader he's taken his "friend" to the motel for lunch.'

'I see,' she said coolly. There was no way that Linda of all people was going to discover how much she was hurting. 'I'm going to have mine in the cabin as I want to make a phone call,' she informed the glamorous nurse in the same calm tones and off she went.

It was something she'd intended doing ever since Sunday's disastrous meeting with Nigel, but every time she thought about it she felt sick. Yet it had to be done. If only for her peace of mind, were she ever to achieve such a state.

When Malcolm's voice came over the line there was just as much pleasure in it as on that other occasion when she'd needed his backing for her job application at the clinic.

'Suzannah!' he said. 'How nice to hear from you again. What can I do for you?'

'You can tell me if you know why Nigel should come seeking me out over here, Malcolm,' she said in subdued tones. 'He turned up out of the blue, suffering from meningitis of all things. Once he was well again he came here on the pretext that he'd like us to get back together again.

'I didn't believe him, and even if I had he was the last person on earth I wanted to see. He made sure that the doctor I work with knew about my past and then flew back to England, but I don't trust him to let the matter drop.'

'The man doesn't change, does he?' Malcolm commented, his voice tightening. 'I can throw some light on what he's been up to but I don't know the full story.'

'I'm listening,' she told him.

'Well, it appears that his overconfidence and carelessness have got him into trouble in the London hospital that he's moved to. Quite serious trouble, I believe, although at the moment it's all very hush-hush. But these recent events have reminded the authorities of what happened with you and, because of Nigel's previous warning, there's now a different school of thought.

'If he'd been able to coax you to go back to him it would have made it seem like a vote of confidence on your part. As we both know, he narrowly missed being suspended when he tried to pin his mistake on you and from what I've heard he needs all the support he can get at the moment. And this time he knows that he's not going to get away with it.'

'Yes, I see,' she said slowly.

'I don't think that Summers can do anything to jeopardise your position with the Newfoundland authorities,' he went on. 'The man is about to lose his credibility. He's treading on eggshells at the moment. I take it that you've made it clear to Dr Hilliard that you were exonerated from any blame?'

Suzannah didn't answer that. She just said gratefully, 'I love you, Malcolm.'

He gave a dry chuckle at the other end of the line. 'I love you too, young Suzannah. Good luck.'

She loved someone else as well, she thought dismally as she replaced the receiver, loved him desperately, and she was sure that he'd felt the same until Nigel had appeared on the scene.

She supposed that the arrogant consultant had done her one favour of sorts. He'd brought her past into the open. Lafe knew all about her now, but it would have been so much better if he'd found out from her. *Why* hadn't she told him before?

Was it because she was a coward? Or because she hadn't wanted to lose his good opinion? A more likely answer was that she would never ever get over the feeling of horror that had swamped her when she'd walked into the ward that day and seen the empty bed.

Ever since, it had been something that she just hadn't been able to talk about. Whenever she'd tried the words had stuck in her throat, and telling Lafe would have been the most difficult thing of all.

But someone else had done it for her. Someone who, from the sound of it, was bad news wherever he went. And the cheek of the man! Trying to coax her back into his life as an insurance against being found incompetent.

As she made a quick snack in what was left of her lunch-hour, Suzannah saw Lafe and Serena come out of his cabin together. He was laughing at something she'd said, looking down at her with amused affection.

Her heart twisted. That was how they had been not so long ago. In tune with each other...in every way. Surely he hadn't found a substitute so soon? She pushed the food away. Suddenly she wasn't hungry.

The motel on the headland had organised a country and western gathering for later in the day, and everyone was going. Even Maisie had produced a battered stetson and a colourful neckerchief in honour of the occasion.

Linda had been flashing high leather boots and a fringed buckskin skirt of very small proportions around the clinic while Shirley, with a suede waistcoat over a colourful shirt and a long denim skirt, looked equally in keeping with the occasion as she prepared to leave in the early evening.

'Aren't you coming?' she asked as Suzannah sat gazing into space.

She shook her head. There was no need to look for an excuse.

She had one already. Over the last week she hadn't had a decent night's sleep. Disturbed nights had been on the agenda. And now, in keeping with her mood, she was going to have an early night.

'Oh, come on, Suzannah,' Shirley coaxed. 'You'll be the only one of us not there.'

'What about Lafe?' she parried. 'He won't be there. He's too engrossed in his lady friend.'

'She's gone. He waved her off an hour ago. It would seem that it was just a flying visit. According to Linda, the eyes and ears of the clinic, Serena stopped off in Port aux Basques to tell him that she's getting married to another of the guys on the ice station. Shopping for a trousseau is what she's been doing.'

'I see.'

'Does that make you feel better, then?' the other woman teased.

She managed a smile. 'A bit. Yes.'

'Only a bit?'

''Fraid so.'

It was true. The news that there was nothing between Lafe and the tiny blonde scientist had taken some of the leaden weight off her mind, but it didn't change anything, did it?

When Shirley had gone she wandered aimlessly around the cabin, too restless to settle to anything. Finally she went to the wardrobe and took out a shirt and pair of trousers. It was ridiculous to sit here moping, she told herself. If Lafe didn't want her company, the others did.

With stylish, high boots on her feet and the soft curtain of her hair swinging beneath a hat that would put Maisie's to shame, she sallied forth and prepared to replace her melancholy with a brittle gaiety.

'So you changed your mind after all!' Shirley cried when she saw her. 'I'm glad that you did, Suzannah. There's little enough goes on around here without missing out on this sort of occasion.'

Suzannah smiled. She liked the uncomplicated physiotherapist and had never regretted agreeing to share a cabin with her. Whereas Linda was a different matter. She was all right on the surface, but Suzannah preferred her in small doses.

At that moment she was behind the microphone in the company of a husky fisherman, belting out a country and western number to the appreciative clapping of the locals.

Alison and Wayne were at a table by themselves, quietly sipping their drinks and keeping a low profile as usual. The only other member of the team was Lafe, and if there was one person she didn't want to think about tonight it was him.

As Shirley pulled out a chair for her, Suzannah looked around the crowded room. Following her gaze, the other woman said, 'Over there...in the corner.'

Lafe was by himself, seated at a table with an untouched drink in front of him and a strange expression on his face.

In a check shirt and jeans that hugged his trim hips like a second skin, he looked very much what he was, an attractive Canadian male. There wouldn't be a woman in the room who hadn't noticed him.

But if that were so, he was showing no interest in anyone, until he looked up and their eyes met. He raised a hand in brief salute but made no attempt to join them.

Suzannah thought glumly that the punishment was continuing. She deserved it...and she was getting it. Why had she come?

A shadow fell across the table and when she looked up Michael Ericson, the lumber-yard manager, was holding out his hand.

'Care to dance, Doc?'

On the point of refusing, Suzannah saw that Lafe was watching them and changed her mind. She would get through to him somehow, she thought. Maybe seeing her in another man's arms would do the trick.

'Yes. Why not?' she said with a dazzling smile for the lumber boss.

The smile was a mistake. He held her too close, and as she wished uncomfortably that it had been a progressive dance that he'd asked her up for, he began to nuzzle her neck with his lips.

They were passing the table where Lafe had been sitting, and her heart sank. He'd gone. Her stupid ploy had got her nowhere other than into an embarrassing situation.

When his voice spoke from behind her she tensed. He must have been following them across the dance floor and she hadn't seen him.

He tapped Michael on the shoulder. 'Excuse me,' he said coolly as he elbowed him out of the way and took her in his arms.

At that moment the call came, 'Swing your partner.' And he did just that. So hard that her feet almost left the floor.

'What was all that about?' he said evenly as she gasped for breath. 'That fellow has slept with every woman for miles around.'

'Really?' she said coldly, stung by the inference that she

wasn't averse to mixing with that type of man. 'And you think that because I was prepared to dance with Michael Ericson, I could be next?'

'Did I say that?' he questioned in the same calm tones. 'I was merely pointing out that give the fellow an inch and he'll take a yard. I thought after Nigel Summers you might be a bit more choosy.'

'Oh, did you?'

She was angry now. Was Lafe blind, or what? Couldn't he see how much she was hurting? Didn't he see that she *had* chosen. She'd chosen *him*...for all time.

All right, it had been a childish thing to do, dazzling the lumber-yard manager, but he'd seemed decent enough that day at the clinic.

If Lafe knew what he'd consulted her about, he would be expecting Michael to ask her to look at his lump again before the night was out...and not from a medical point of view.

And did Lafe have to be so blandly reproving? His tone was more like that of a parent with a wayward child than a jealous lover.

Suzannah had a sinking feeling that he'd written her off. That his intervention in the middle of the dance had been merely that of an acquaintance bent on saving her from herself.

At that moment the music stopped. Infuriating her still further, he said, 'I've been wondering if there's anything else you haven't told me about yourself.'

'Such as what?' she hissed angrily. 'That I'm married with six children? I chew tobacco? I've got a birthmark in a certain place? But you'd know about that, wouldn't you?

'I think you need to understand one thing, Lafe,' she went on. 'I admit that I've been less than truthful with you. I kept it from you that I knew Nigel when he put in an appearance and, yes, I didn't tell you about the trouble back home, but it was because I've felt totally vulnerable ever since it happened. Not because I'm guilty of any crime.

'It was because of that vulnerability that I came to stay with John and Debbie, to get away from the pain and shame that I'd had to endure back home. I couldn't stand the thought of any more censure, especially from you. So now you have it.'

She paused for breath and he took the opportunity to interrupt. 'That may all be true, and as we doctors are only human I don't condemn you for a mistake. It's your lack of honesty that hurts. We had your ex-fiancé here at Bramble Bay, but did you inform me of the fact? You'd been in trouble back home, but did you trust me enough to tell me about it…even though you say you were blameless? I recommended you for the post here in Bramble Bay, don't forget, and that's how you repay me.'

Suzannah looked around her. She'd been desperate to talk to him ever since Nigel's cruel revelation, and where had they ended up having a heart to heart? On the edge of a dance floor in a wooden hut.

A decision that she should have made days ago was forming in her mind, and whether or not it was the right place to inform him of it, she was going to do so.

'I'm leaving, Lafe,' she said with quiet despair. 'It's the obvious thing to do. I should never have come here in the first place.'

She watched his jaw tighten and the chill in his frank blue gaze deepen. 'You're not just going to slope off when it pleases you, Suzannah,' he snapped. 'The terms of your contract state that you have to work a month's notice.'

'All right! I'll do that!' she flared. 'And then I'm off.'

'So be it,' he remarked grimly. Inclining his head dismissively, he went back to his solitary table in the corner.

'What was all that about?' Shirley asked curiously as she

slumped down onto her seat. 'You both looked very serious.'

'Just tying up a few loose ends,' Suzannah told her evasively.

There was no point in telling any of the others that she was leaving until nearer the time. If Lafe wanted to inform them, that was up to him, but as far as she was concerned it was between the two of them only.

So that was it, Lafe thought as he drove back to the clinic. He was driving her away. Suzannah couldn't stand the sight of him any longer.

Why was he being so unforgiving? It wasn't in his nature to be so, but he'd never felt so let down in the whole of his life.

If it had been anyone else it wouldn't have mattered, but his beautiful English doctor had been less than honest with him. It hurt that she hadn't trusted him enough to confide in him.

What his course of action would have been if she had, he wasn't sure, but they would have surmounted the problems together. Instead, she'd kept the matter to herself and in so doing had made him feel that their relationship was a farce.

When she'd thrown the threat of resignation at him he'd clutched at the nearest straw and reminded her that she was required to work a month's notice.

Why, he didn't rightly know. He could have persuaded the authorities to waive it, but in that moment all he'd been able to think of was that he couldn't let her go with this barrier between them.

His instincts told him that Suzannah wouldn't stay on in Newfoundland after what had happened. She would go back home and he would be left to carry on the aimless life that had been his before he'd met her.

She'd left the motel before the rest of them, and when he got back to Bramble Bay her cabin was in darkness. He stood motionless in the snow, eyeing its unlighted windows. Was she asleep already? Calmer, now that she'd made the decision?

CHAPTER NINE

IT WAS done. Suzannah had tendered her resignation and it had been accepted by the health authority at Port aux Basques. There had been some surprise at the shortness of her stay at the satellite clinic, but as that fact had given her little chance to make an impression on them, there had been no persuasion regarding a rethink.

Lafe's comments had been quietly condemning. 'So you're determined to let us down? It was fortunate for the folks of Newfoundland and Labrador that your hero Wilfred Grenfell had a bit more staying power.'

'Don't make out that my presence in the clinic means that much,' she'd said with a defiant toss of her head. 'You'll soon replace me...in every way. I shall be paying for my mistakes the rest of my life. It's something that I accept. What I don't want to have to put up with is your continuing disapproval. I admit that I deserve it, but I did have my reasons.'

That had been the moment when he could have made a gesture to mend matters, but he hadn't. He'd just observed her with the guarded expression that he was adopting whenever they were together and said, 'Are you intending going back to England?'

'I might. There's nothing to keep me here. John and his family have their own lives to lead and I ought to do the same.'

'What?'

'Get a life.'

'What about Summers?' he asked grimly.

'What about him?'

'He still wants you, doesn't he?'

'Nigel always wants what he can't have.'

'I see. So why don't you tell me what really happened? Trust me for once. Instead of feeding me morsels of it when the mood takes you, tell me the whole story.'

Suzannah swallowed hard.

'Nigel decided to take a very sick child off steroids and I let him. He'd been partying and was furious to have been called away. I protested, insisting that it wasn't safe to do it so abruptly. That annoyed him even more and he sent me packing. When the child died, he and the nurse that I'd left him with said that I'd crossed the steroids off the drug sheet.

'Because he was the hospital's "golden boy", he was believed and I was only cleared when the nurse, who fancied him a lot, decided that she'd been used.'

'Summers set you up. You did nothing wrong,' he breathed.

'Not exactly,' she told him, her face whitening at the memory. 'Somehow or other I should have stopped him.' And with her eyes awash with tears she left him to his thoughts.

They were chaotic ones. Ever since the country and western night at the motel Lafe had felt as if he wasn't thinking straight.

She'd flung at him that she was leaving and he'd been totally dismayed at his handling of the situation, but now his mind was absolutely reeling.

That rat's part in the affair was something else that Suzannah had kept to herself, he thought, but this time he had to admire her for it. Though it still rankled that she hadn't felt close enough to him to tell him the whole story.

As he went to face those needing the services of the clinic he consoled himself with the thought that Suzannah wasn't going yet.

He wasn't going to allow her to depart even one day before her month's notice had been completed. If he hadn't got the rift between them healed before then it would be no one's fault but his own.

As the bleak mantle of winter settled itself more firmly on Newfoundland and Labrador, Suzannah marvelled at the hardiness of the people.

The cold was intense but they accepted it without complaining. She supposed it was because they were accustomed to it, as were the lumbering moose and fleet-footed caribou. For her own part, she felt as if she would never be warm again, and it wasn't just the season that was to blame.

She'd come to Newfoundland to get away from the misery of her life in England, putting her career on hold until she'd decided where her future lay.

On a mellow day in autumn she'd got her answer. She'd met a blond Viking with easy charm and unassuming integrity and had known that nothing was ever going to be the same again.

Falling in love with Lafe had been as inevitable as night following day, but the last thing she'd visualised had been working with him in the wilds of Newfoundland, practising medicine in the country that she'd escaped to.

Because of that she'd kept her past to herself. Wrongly, as it had turned out, but the deed was done and all that remained was to work out her notice and go.

She would return to England. If she stayed on in St Anthony with John and Debbie there would always be the chance of meeting Lafe, and to continue the charade of being merely casual acquaintances was more than she would be able to cope with.

If his anger had persisted she might have felt better, but apart from his display of annoyance at her coming departure now he was just blandly aloof all the time, and that was the hardest thing to bear.

On a cold morning in late November a party of teenage skiers who had been coursing down a neighbouring slope came to the clinic with one of their number who had lost control and hit a tree. The lad hadn't been going at top speed, but when Suzannah saw him he had facial bruising, possible wrist fractures and was in shock.

The leader of the party, an extremely confident student, seemed to be more interested in making his own presence felt than showing concern for the injured youth.

'Hi, Doc,' he said. 'Old Mikey here has gone and hit a tree. We've all been at the wine, I'm afraid.' As she motioned for them to help the injured youth onto the couch he looked around him. 'Cosy place you've got here. I'd have done myself some mischief if I'd known there was going to be a babe like you in attendance.'

'Will you all, please, go back into the waiting room?' she said as she bent over the patient. 'This young man is in shock, as well as being injured.'

The damaged wrists had the appearance of Colles' fractures. Along with his hands, they were displaced backwards which indicated that the lower ends of the radii were broken. He had obviously slammed up against the tree with both hands raised, and they'd taken the brunt of the impact.

The pushy one was in the doorway again. 'Any chance of a coffee?' he wanted to know.

Suzannah shook her head without speaking. Maisie wasn't around and there was no way that she was going to oblige.

She was propping up the injured youth's legs so that they were higher than his body and covering him with blankets to reduce heat loss, while thinking that the other guy hadn't been wrong about the wine. She could smell it on his breath quite clearly.

So far the lad hadn't spoken. His breathing was shallow and he moaned constantly with the pain. While she was phoning for an ambulance Suzannah looked up and saw that the pest was back.

'If you don't stay out of the way while I'm attending to your friend, I'll have you ejected from the clinic,' she threatened.

'And who's going to do that?' he asked impudently, reaching forward to tweak her hair at the same time.

'I am,' Lafe told him from the doorway of the small consulting room. 'Your friend is badly injured and Dr Scott is trying to assess his injuries. Get back to your mates and stay there.'

'All right,' he sneered. 'No need to get snarly. If this is how you treat your patients I'm glad it's not me.'

'Look, sonny,' Lafe told him, 'just go and behave yourself, and next time you all go skiing keep off the wine.'

When he'd gone slouching off Lafe came across and, placing his arm across her shoulders, he held her for a second.

'You all right?' he asked with his face only inches from hers.

Suzannah nodded. 'Yes. He was a pain but that was all. I've dealt with worse than that in the past.'

She was so conscious of Lafe's nearness that she couldn't breathe. It was the first time he'd touched her in weeks, and it was as if she, too, had been on the wine. She felt drunk with the surprise of the moment.

And then what had she done? Mentioned the past! It was the last thing she needed to remind him of, and as she dragged her eyes away from his steady blue gaze she knew that nothing had changed.

It was merely a moment of one colleague being protective of another, and she almost wished that she'd been in real danger so that she might have been the object of his concern to a greater degree.

He was putting her away from him and bending over the young skier. 'Ambulance on its way?' he asked.

Suzannah nodded and pointing to the wrists. 'Colles' fractures, would you say?'

'Looks like it. Life won't be all that easy if he ends up with them both in plaster.'

He looked up suddenly. 'When this young fellow has been picked up, I'd like a word.'

'What about?' she asked quickly.

'Later,' he said as Linda came in to clean up the cuts and scratches on the patient's face.

'Later' turned out to be that evening. A knock on the cabin door as she and Shirley were clearing up after their evening meal produced Lafe on the step.

'Are you free to come over to my place?' he asked abruptly, after a smiling nod in Shirley's direction.

'Er...yes, I suppose so.'

Suzannah had been wondering all day what it was he wanted to discuss, and now she was about to find out.

It was a cold, clear night, and as they walked across the crisp snow that was ever-present Suzannah's heartbeat was quickening. Was Lafe going to tell her that she was forgiven? she wondered. Or was it a vain hope?

She was shivering and not just with the cold. Nigel had a lot to answer for, but telling Lafe about her disastrous past was the worst thing he'd done to her.

'Sit down, Suzannah,' he said, pulling a chair up to the stove.

When she'd obeyed the request, he stood looking down at her with the veiled expression that drove her crazy. She'd been used to his candid blue gaze being the mirror of his mind, but it wasn't like that any more.

'You're two weeks into your notice, aren't you?' he said at last.

'Yes, and I don't need to be reminded of the fact,' she said stiffly, deciding that he could make of that what he wanted.

'I mention it only because Christmas will be just a couple of weeks away when you leave here. Had you thought of that?'

'Christmas!' she echoed blankly. 'No, as a matter of fact, I hadn't. I can't think of anything that's been further from my mind.'

'So you haven't decided where you'll be spending it?'

'No. But it won't be with John and Debbie. They're going to friends in Vancouver for Christmas.'

'Maybe you'll be back in England by then.'

'Why are you asking me all these questions when in reality you don't care a damn where I'll be, or what I'm doing?'

She watched his jawline tighten and longed to touch the face that was always in her mind.

'I was about to say that if you haven't made any plans, why not extend your notice and stay on here until the New Year? It would be better than being at a loose end.'

'Oh! So that's it,' she cried. 'You see me as little orphan Annie! Well, I'm not a charity case. Don't develop a guilt complex on my behalf, Lafe. I've asked for all I've got and I'm accepting it. Where I spend Christmas isn't your concern. At this moment it isn't mine either but, no doubt, I will sort something out once I've left Bramble Bay. I take it that the others still don't know that I'm going?'

'Correct. That's what we agreed, isn't it?'

'Yes, it's what we agreed,' she said with sudden weariness, 'and now, if that's all you want me for, I'll be off.'

He nodded. 'Yes, that's it, except for one thing.'

'What's that?'

'Have you had any feedback from England? Any news from your friend Malcolm Stennet?'

She shook her head. 'No. Nothing since I phoned him just after Nigel's departure. At that time he said that Nigel was in deep trouble, and as he hadn't been able to persuade me to take up where we left off, Malcolm didn't think that I'd hear anything else from him. And if I do, it doesn't matter now as I'm going.

'You once reminded me that you'd put your reputation on the line when you recommended me, and I'd let you down. Well, now you're off the hook. Or at least you will be once I've gone.'

Her smile was full of wry sadness as she turned to go. 'What a pity I turned out to be such a bad risk.'

'That's not the case, Suzannah,' he said quietly. 'I've seen you work. You're a good doctor. One of the best. All right, you were involved in something very upsetting and you've paid for it with the loss of your peace of mind. It's the fact that you didn't feel you could confide in me that—'

Suzannah held up her hand to stop him. 'I know. You've already told me. Goodnight, Lafe.'

He took a step towards her and she knew that the atmosphere had changed. The chemistry between them, which she'd thought to be dead, was fusing again. There was a look on his face that she'd seen before in the days when she'd realised that it had taken a trip to faraway Newfoundland to find the man she would love for ever.

But what was the point? As she turned away from sweet temptation it was with the knowledge that without love and respect there was no future for them.

Closing the door quickly behind her, Suzannah looked up into a starlit sky. In this cold, white world she'd come to, it seemed as if her life was the only thing that was grey.

So much for that, Lafe thought bleakly as the door closed behind her. His ploy to get Suzannah to stay longer hadn't worked, and he supposed it wasn't surprising. He'd rubbed her up the wrong way the moment he'd opened his mouth. She'd angrily compared herself to little orphan Annie and it had gone on from there.

Yet all he wanted was to keep her here. The thought of her alone and desolate over the festive season was more than he could bear. So why wasn't he doing something positive about it?

He nearly had done in those last few seconds before she'd left. As Suzannah had stood before him, desire had risen in him in an overwhelming tide. The memory of when they'd slept together had been there in his mind. The beauty of her lissom nakedness in his arms. The way she'd given herself to him without making any demands. Wanting only to please him.

But he'd read her mind as she'd left. She'd picked up on the ache in him and had decided, rightly so, that the one wasn't right without the other. She'd thought that it had all changed. That now he merely lusted after her. They were going backwards and all because he'd denied her the right to human frailty.

Local women were attending for smear tests the following afternoon, grateful that the facility was now more readily available since the setting up of the clinic.

Suzannah and the two nurses were kept busy as they came and went, and it was only as they were clearing away after the last one had departed that they had the chance to discuss other matters than medical ones.

'Guess what?' Linda said as they prepared to go their separate ways.

The other two eyed her enquiringly.

'What?' Wayne asked warily.

'It's somebody's birthday today.'

'Whose?' Suzannah questioned.

'Lafe's.'

'How do you know?' she asked slowly.

'There was mail for him this morning, a couple of envelopes that obviously held cards. When I asked him he said, yes, it was his birthday, and that the cards were from the folks on the ice station where he'd been working.'

'He didn't seem very excited about the event so I suggested that we all congregate at the motel tonight for a drink. How are you folks fixed?'

Wayne nodded and Suzannah said, 'Yes, of course. I'd no idea.'

'Good. We'll say about eightish, shall we?' Linda suggested. 'I'll go and tell him that we're all for it.'

As she walked back to her cabin Suzannah wondered if Lafe would be expecting her to be there. As a member of staff, yes. As someone now on the perimeter of his life, no.

She wished she'd known it was his birthday. They'd had that strained meeting at his place the previous night and he'd never mentioned it. But, then, he wouldn't, would he? If Lafe celebrated his birthday at all, he would want it to be with folks he was comfortable with and she didn't come into that category.

Nevertheless, she was going to go. Every second spent with him was precious. What was more, she was going to make her presence felt. In the doghouse she might be, but if Lafe couldn't forget her past misdemeanours, *she* would...for tonight at least.

There was no country and western music blasting forth tonight, just a comfortable and relaxed atmosphere under soft lights that made the cold grip of winter outside seem less restricting.

Lafe was already there, as were the rest of the clinic staff, including the redoubtable Maisie, and when Suzannah walked across to the small group at a table in the corner all eyes were on her.

He was seated next to Linda with his arm draped across the back of her chair, smiling at something she'd just said, but when he saw Suzannah appear he got to his feet.

'Suzannah,' he said easily, as if they were the best of friends. 'We'd almost given you up.'

She noticed that it was 'we', not 'I'. Lafe was at pains to make her see that she was just one of the group.

Her eyes were clear and untroubled, her smile wide, as she acknowledged his greeting.

'Surely you didn't think I would miss an occasion such as your birthday,' she said lightly, adding with a husky laugh, 'I've even put on my best frock.'

There was no lack of warm appraisal in the glance that he was bestowing upon her and, joining in the charade, he countered, 'So I see. I'm honoured.'

The frock that she'd referred to was a low-cut black dress of soft wool that clung to her slender curves just enough to spell out the promise of what lay beneath. With it she was wearing high-heeled black shoes, which she'd changed into on arriving at the motel, and a silver necklace and earrings completed a picture of elegance.

Suzannah was conscious of Linda's irritation as Lafe pulled out a chair for her, and she hid a smile. The other woman obviously thought that, having arranged the little get-together, she was entitled to his full attention, and Suzannah's late arrival had interrupted their little tête-à-tête.

Another time she might have felt bad, but not tonight. When she made her ignominious departure in a couple of weeks' time, the flashy nurse would have him all to herself for as long as she wanted, she thought grimly, but tonight was hers.

As the evening progressed she could tell that Lafe was puzzled by her attitude. Having temporarily thrown off the mantle of the repressed sinner, she was dazzling.

Her dark eyes glowed every time their glances met. Her lips had a sweet curving message for him alone. As his gaze took in the smooth, while column of her throat and the high, thrusting breasts beneath it, the ache that only Suzannah aroused in him was increasing with every second.

'What are you trying to do, Suzannah?' he growled when the attention of the others was momentarily diverted. 'Seduce me by remote control? You're trying to prove a point, aren't you?'

'Maybe.'

'Well, you've succeeded. Let's leave the others to it. You go first and I'll follow on behind.'

Suddenly it wasn't exciting any more. Hadn't she told herself countless times that desire without love wasn't enough? Lafe deserved better than this.

His bright blue gaze was cooling, as if he knew what was coming next, but the moment was fragmented as the outer doors of the motel were flung open and on the blast of an icy wind a man came staggering in.

'There's an almighty blizzard out there! Conditions are worsenin' fast!' he gasped, pointing over his shoulder. 'Those kids who wuz hangin' around earlier have gone back up the mountain.'

The two doctors froze, their own problems forgotten in the anxiety of the moment. The same thought was in both their minds. Surely the pushy student and his friends hadn't gone back on the slopes after what had happened to the other lad.

Newfoundland was a country where the weather could change in seconds, but to a dangerous degree. It had been a clear, cold night as she'd driven to the headland where the motel was situated but now, from all accounts, there were hazardous conditions outside.

'How do you know they're up there?' Lafe asked as they all gathered round the man.

'Saw 'em goin' up minutes after the ambulance left with one of their mates,' he told them. 'It was sunny then but, buddy, it sure ain't now!'

'Right, then,' a burly individual in a sheepskin jacket said. 'We'd best get in touch with the police and the rescue teams. Folks have frozen to death before now in this kind of weather.'

Suzannah shuddered. The thought of the carefree lads stiff and cold at the bottom of some crevasse didn't bear thinking of.

'I'm going back to get supplies from the clinic and to change my clothes, then I'm joining the search party,' Lafe said abruptly. 'They might need medical help when they locate them.'

'I'm going with you.'

'No! You're not! It's too risky.'

Suzannah eyed him frostily. 'I've climbed the Welsh mountains back home many a time.'

'Not in these sorts of weather conditions, I'd like to bet. You're in Newfoundland now,' he said tightly. 'And we treat the weather with respect in this country. I've gone up there as back-up for the rescue teams many a time and it's no joke.'

'So? There has to be a first time for everything and this can be my first. I'm going with you no matter what you say!'

She wasn't going to tell Lafe that the thought of him risking his life up there on the mountains would only be bearable if she was there, too.

'All right,' he agreed grimly, 'but don't blame me if you

lose parts of your anatomy from frostbite. It can happen, you know. Fingers, toes…'

'All right. So what? I've already lost my heart,' she said recklessly, thinking that he could make what he would of that.

'Now you're being flippant,' he growled, 'but it's not the time or place to go into that. If you're coming with me you'll need to get changed, too, so we'd best be off.'

This was the limit, he was thinking grimly. Only minutes ago Suzannah and he had been about to leave. The deadlock between them had been on the point of breaking as their longing for each other had surfaced again during the evening and they'd been desperate to be alone.

And what had happened? Those crazy kids had gone back up the mountain in spite of one of their number already having been injured. Admittedly, the weather had been fair when they'd gone up, but the climate could change violently from one moment to the next, as was the case today, and all the locals present were aware that the youngsters could be in grave danger.

While he and Suzannah had been talking, the local men were discussing what action to take. The burly fellow who'd elected himself spokesman when the situation arose had gone to phone the rescue services, and some of the others were contemplating setting off up the slopes themselves.

'It'll take a while for any rescue units to get here,' the man said when he came back from phoning, 'so some of us might as well set off. After all, we probably know the mountain better than they do.'

As there was a murmur of agreement he turned to the two doctors. 'You guys are from the clinic, ain't yer?'

'Yes,' Lafe told him, 'and we're coming with you. The lads might need medical attention when we find them.'

'*If* we find them,' a mournful voice said from the back of the group.

'Well, there's one thing fer sure,' the big one said. 'We ain't goin' to find 'em standin' around here. We'll meet up again in half an hour…an' be dressed and ready fer off.'

As she drove back to the clinic to change, Suzannah could see the headlamps of the Shogun lighting up the road behind her, and she thought wryly that it had to take an emergency such as this for them to be together.

Though Lafe didn't appear to see it in that light. He'd made it clear that he didn't want her with him. Maybe she'd imagined that he'd been desperate for her company earlier in the evening.

Perhaps he'd no wish to be with her for any length of time since his change of heart, and lengthy was what this state of affairs might turn out to be.

When she presented herself at his door a short time later the glamorous seductress of earlier had been replaced with a muffled figure in a woolly hat pulled down well over her ears, a heavy waxed jacket, warm trousers and sturdy walking boots.

If Lafe had been feeling less grim he might have found himself smiling at the contrast, but the evening had turned into something very worrying and Suzannah wasn't helping things by insisting on going with him up the mountain.

'Here, take this,' he said, handing her a medium-sized rucksack. 'It's got medical supplies inside.' He pointed to a huge bag at his feet. 'And the rest are in here. Unfortunately, I haven't been able to lay my hands on anything to replace a lost heart, but I'll give the matter some thought the first chance I get.'

Suzannah glared at him. Whatever had possessed her to say such a thing?

'As the article in question belongs to me, I think that it's up to me to retrieve it from the limbo that it's now wallowing in. Thanks just the same,' she said stiffly, thinking as she did so that it was a ridiculous cat-and-mouse-type conversation they were having.

'Maybe so,' he said equably as he ushered her towards the car. 'We'll discuss it another time, eh? Those young guys on the mountain are our priority at the moment.'

She nodded. Lafe was right. They had no right to be babbling on about their own affairs when a group of teenagers were in danger.

But maybe by the time they got back to the motel they would have turned up and the panic would be over, she thought optimistically.

It wasn't to be. There was no sign of the missing youths when they got back to the motel, just a group of solemn-faced men about to set off on an unpleasant outing.

'They're going to send a helicopter out, but the weather will have to improve before they'll risk it,' one of the men said. 'And as there's no sign of it and we don't want to waste any time, we're setting off now. Are you folks all geared up?'

The two doctors nodded and Lafe told him, 'We'll bring up the rear. We're both carrying medical supplies and don't want to risk losing them, so we'll let you lead the way.'

Within minutes they were off, a file of volunteers moving slowly up the first slopes, their outlines showing darkly through the swirling snow, in a wind with a bite that took the breath away and stung the cheeks.

As Suzannah and Lafe prepared to follow them he was telling himself that he was insane to have let her get involved in this. How could it be happening?

Supposing they died up here on the mountain and he'd never told her that the only thing that mattered to him in the world was that she be safe and happy.

That was a laugh! She was anything but. Safe she wasn't

out here in the awful weather conditions, and he'd made darned sure that she wasn't happy.

If the boot had been on the other foot, would he have wanted to tell her that he'd once been involved in the needless death of a patient?

He'd told her about what had happened with his sister and she'd been totally supportive, but they'd both known that his guilt over that had been an overreaction to grief. In Suzannah's case, the chance had been there and she hadn't taken it...and was he making things any better for her? No!

She was eyeing him questioningly. 'If we don't get a move on they'll be out of sight, and we'll be no use to anyone if we get lost, too.'

He nodded grimly. She was right. This was no time for self-analysis.

CHAPTER TEN

THE higher they climbed the colder it became, and as the possible consequences of the expedition plagued their minds Suzannah and Lafe battled on, grim-faced and silent.

He was horrified that he'd let her get involved in this, while she was trying to keep at bay terrifying visions of what might have happened to those they were searching for.

The men leading the way up the mountain plodded doggedly on, shouting all the time, hoping for an answer, but there was none. The lights they were carrying weren't strong enough to illuminate more than a few yards at a time and nothing or no one came into view.

Suddenly there was a cry of 'Halt!' As they all came to a stop, those at the front pointed to a narrow crevasse almost at their feet.

'There's one of 'em down there!' one of the men cried. 'I can see his dark jacket outlined against the snow.'

As they all peered down into the chasm, Suzannah said with her eyes on Lafe, 'He isn't moving. Do you think he's unconseious?'

'I've no idea,' he said tersely. 'And as the opening is too narrow for any of us to get down to him, we're not likely to find out.'

'I can,' she said immediately. 'I'm slim enough to get down there.'

'Forget it!' he snapped. 'I'm already having a fit at you being exposed to this weather. The last thing I'm going to allow you to do is endanger your life even more.'

'You don't own me!' she flared back. 'Stop telling me what I can and can't do.'

'Quiet!' he barked. 'I thought I heard him.'

He was right. It came again. A faint cry for help.

'I'm going down to him,' she told him, 'and while I'm gone, the rest of you need to look around for the others. They can't be far away.'

'Who's giving the orders now?' Lafe snarled. Lowering his voice even more so that only she could hear, he said, 'Have you got a death wish, Suzannah?'

'Might have,' she flipped back. And without giving him chance to comment further, she called to the rest of the searchers, 'I'm going down to him. Fasten a rope around me.'

There was silence as her words sank in and then without more ado they began to do as she asked while Lafe looked on in stony disbelief.

Someone thrust a torch into her hands and someone else a blanket, and as she stood poised on the edge Suzannah took one last look at Lafe.

She wanted to tell him she loved him...desperately. That he was everything she'd ever wanted and if she didn't get out of this alive...

Instead she cried, 'Throw the rucksack down to me when I get to the bottom, Lafe. There isn't room for me to descend with it on my back.'

He nodded grimly and she thought with sudden despair, I can't ever do anything right for him. What does he expect me to do? Leave the lad down there?

As they lowered her over the edge his face was the last thing she saw, and there was no comfort to be had from it. She understood his feelings up to a point. He was used to being the one to take risks and he was having to stand to one side while she played superwoman.

But really! He might at least have told her to take care.

Or held her for a moment before she began her descent. But it was as if she was out to annoy him deliberately.

Lafe considered himself a reasonable man, but as he watched Suzannah disappear from view he could barely contain himself. He'd let her come on the rescue mission much against his better judgement.

But as they'd argued the pros and cons it hadn't seemed the right moment to tell her that the thought of anything happening to her made his blood run cold, so he'd let her persuade him to take her along.

As the weather had worsened his misgivings had increased, but it had been nothing compared to this. Only minutes ago they'd been trudging up the mountain side and now…!

Now Suzannah was being lowered down the narrow crevasse at their feet, while he had to look on and watch in a state of anxiety so acute he thought his heart would stop beating. He wasn't used to being the bystander, but on this occasion he had no choice.

'Keep the rope taut,' he said urgently as Suzannah braced herself against the sides of the opening with her feet. 'If it's too slack Dr Scott will swing against the side and injure herself on the rock. If that happens we could end up with two of them down there.'

Where the dickens were the rescue services and the helicopter? he thought desperately. At that moment one of the men cried, 'Look! Here's the rest of the kids!'

Lafe looked up to see an exhausted band of youngsters approaching, their movements slow and laboured, their faces blue with the cold. As some of the locals hurried towards them, Lafe prayed that Suzannah and the lad in the crevasse would be as fortunate.

It was deeper than Suzannah had thought. The torch she was carrying told her that, and by the time she'd got to the bottom of the narrow ravine she was scratched and bruised all over.

When she finally reached the injured youth there was barely room to stand without treading on him. After his feeble cry for help it appeared that he'd lapsed into unconsciousness as there was no response when she spoke to him.

However, his pulse seemed strong enough and his heartbeat was regular. But for how long? she thought.

There was blood seeping through his woolly hat and one of his legs was bent in an awkward position. Those were visible injuries. There could be others not yet seen but, except for injecting him to deaden the pain that would soon penetrate his unconsciousness, there was little she could do in the confined space.

It was vital to get him raised to the top so that his condition could be assessed properly. Looking up into the white blurs that were the faces of those above, she called, 'I'm going to need a backboard and a surgical collar. Is there any sign of the helicopter? He's unconscious and bleeding from the head...and there's a lot of loose rock skittering down here from above.'

Lafe shuddered. That was all they needed. A rockfall! It had stopped snowing and miraculously the wind had dropped, but now there was another hazard to contend with...falling rock!

The answer to her question was no, the helicopter hadn't yet appeared, but as the blizzard had stopped as quickly as it had started, it should be on its way.

Some of the men were helping the other boys down the mountainside, and it was left to Lafe and those who remained to huddle anxiously around the top of the crevasse, their ears straining for the sound of the helicopter.

At last it came—the whirring of blades in the clear night sky—and within seconds a helicopter was landing on a small plateau nearby.

'My colleague wants a backboard sent down,' Lafe told them with rough urgency as the paramedics came spilling out. 'There's an injured lad down there, and once she's managed to get him onto it we can haul him up...and then do the same for her.'

'Her!' the guy in charge was exclaiming. 'It's a woman down there? My nerves!'

'Exactly,' the fair-haired doctor gritted. 'So let's get moving, shall we?'

The boy was up. Lafe was examining him after a slow, nerve-stretching haul up the crevasse. The fact that he'd been unconscious had made a difficult task a bit easier as there had been no struggles on his part as the ascent had been made. But his face and hands were scratched where they'd brushed against the rock and altogether he was a sorry sight.

Fortunately he'd been wearing a heavy padded jacket, which had protected the top half of his body, and Suzannah had used a length of cord that she'd found in the rucksack to tie one of the blankets around his legs.

'He's got head injuries and possible fractures,' Lafe informed the paramedics who'd come with the helicopter. 'The sooner we get him to hospital the better.'

They were already preparing to stretcher the youth to the waiting chopper and the pilot said, 'You're lucky that the weather straightened out, otherwise we wouldn't have been able to take to the air. Even in these improved conditions we're not keen on making this sort of journey.'

His eyes were on the men around the edge of the crevasse as he said flatly, 'There'll be the lady, too. We'll have to come back for her as she ain't gonna have come through this mess unscratched.'

Lafe was already running back to join the others now

that the boy was in safe hands, and the pilot's words did nothing to ease the anxiety that was tearing at him.

After the freezing conditions up above it had been warm in the hollow down in the mountain, and as Suzannah struggled into the harness that had been thrown down to her she was experiencing a strange reluctance to go back aloft. Not because she wasn't aware of the dangers of the situation, but because there, in the bowels of the mountain, she didn't have to answer to anybody but herself.

Ever since arriving in Bramble Bay, she and Lafe had been 'doctors on ice' and not just geographically. Their relationship had become a cold, frozen thing and she thought with sudden drowsiness that she didn't want to go back up there to be chilled off again.

'Are you ready, ma'am?' a voice called, echoing eerily down the split in the mountainside. 'If you are, give a pull on the rope.'

Suzannah looked down on to the thick coil slotted through the harness. You can't stay down here, you crazy woman, she told herself. You've done enough hiding away already. And with a quick tug on the rope she prepared for lift-off.

It was as she raised her head in the act of bracing herself for movement that the biggest rock fragment so far came bouncing purposefully down towards her. As she cowered back, unable to move out of its path, it struck her on the temple.

'The doctor's been hit by falling rock!' somebody cried as Lafe joined them at the edge of the opening, and as a gasp of dismay went up his face blanched.

'Let me see!' he cried. Pushing his way to the front, he peered down the hole.

He could see Suzannah swaying on the end of the rope and for the first time in his life Lafe cursed his size. He was unable to get to her and she needed him...desperately.

'Bring her up!' he commanded. 'We brought the lad up safely in an unconscious state and we're going to have to do the same for the doctor. But, for God's sake, watch what you're doing. Don't harm her any more than she is already.'

'OK, Doc,' the man in charge of the rescue team said calmly. 'Best not look while it's being done, eh?'

Lafe glared at him. 'If there was enough space I'd be down there with her…never mind not being able to watch!' he bellowed.

He was in the middle of a nightmare. If anything happened to Suzannah before he'd told her… Don't think about it, he told himself raggedly. It'll be time to start planning the future when she's out of this hell pit.

After what seemed like a lifetime of carefully easing the rope upwards, with Suzannah's limp body dangling loosely from the end of it, eager hands, his own foremost, were able to reach out for her.

As they brought her over the edge of the crevasse onto the snow-covered slope of the mountain, Lafe's heartbeats were like thunder in his ears. 'Stand back, everyone…please, while I examine Dr Scott,' he ordered brusquely.

He was lifting her eyelids and shining a small torch onto the pupils, then feeling her head where the rockfall had knocked her senseless.

A gash on her cheek was bleeding and the flesh on her temple was beginning to swell. It felt soft and squelchy to the touch, and he knew that they had to get Suzannah to hospital as quickly as possible.

He looked around him desperately. How long was the helicopter going to be? The guy had said he'd be right back after depositing the youngsters, but the hospital was a heck of a way off.

In what seemed a reasonably short time, those on the

mountainside heard the whirring of blades once more and Lafe let out a sigh of relief.

If Suzannah was bleeding inside the cranium as well as outside, speed was of the essence. That, and the extreme cold in her present condition, could kill her. But that was something he daren't dwell on. He should never have let her persuade him to take her along.

They were certainly a pair of guilt-trippers, he told himself grimly. He'd just about come to terms with the part he'd played—or hadn't played—in his sister's tragedy, and now he might be on the edge of another heartbreaking loss.

And the limp figure now being carefully placed in the helicopter had bravely endured the result of a lapse that she would always regret, but which hadn't been her fault.

Don't let Suzannah die! Lafe pleaded of an unseen deity, but the only answer was the raised voices of the rescuers as they prepared to make their tortuous way back down the mountainside.

'I'm coming with you,' he told the helicopter crew.

They eyed him doubtfully.

'We've got a full house,' the pilot told him. 'I don't think there's going to be room.'

Lafe nodded bleakly. 'All right. I'll follow on somehow or other, but be sure that the staff at the other end know about the possibility of haemorrhaging in the skull. Dr Scott will need immediate treatment.'

Letting Suzannah out of his care was going to be a fitting end to a horrendous night, he thought grimly as the helicopter began to rise skywards. But there was no arguing with the logic of what the man had said, and as long as Suzannah was on her way to hospital he would have to be satisfied with that. It would be a long journey by car and the sooner he was on his way the better.

As the helicopter made its way through the cold night sky Suzannah regained consciousness. Her first thoughts were that she was moving and the noise of propeller blades told her in what.

A young paramedic was bending over her, and as she met his concerned gaze she whispered weakly, 'Lafe? Where is he?'

'The other doc?' he said. When she nodded painfully, he said, '*He's* still on the mountain and *you're* going to Port aux Basques. It was a mighty brave thing you did back there, lady. The kid's already in Intensive Care and we're going to get somebody to look at your head as soon as we get there. The other doctor was dead keen that we should get that sorted.'

Suzannah raised her hand and touched the side of her temple carefully. It was there, the soft squelchy mass that indicated bleeding inside the dura mater.

She closed her eyes to hide the tears that were threatening. If he was so concerned about her, why wasn't Lafe here?

A CT scan had shown that there was indeed an extradural haemorrhage present, caused by the falling rock, and Suzannah knew enough about such situations to be prepared for the surgery that would follow.

A craniotomy would have to be carried out, which meant the surgeons at Port aux Basques drilling burr holes in her skull to drain away the blood that was collecting. Then the ruptured blood vessels would be clipped off to prevent further bleeding and hopefully that would be the end of it.

It was a situation that could be life-threatening if not treated quickly, and as she was prepared for Theatre it was hard not to ask herself what her chances were.

If only Lafe were here with his cool confidence and calm strength, she thought miserably, but he'd done his bit back there on the mountain by urging them to see to her head...and he had a clinic to run, didn't he? It couldn't all fall apart because one of his staff had been injured.

She managed a watery smile at the thought of their expressions when they heard about the rescue of the foolish teenagers. Linda would be sorry that she'd missed all the excitement.

As they wheeled her down to Theatre the thought came to mind that her stay in hospital would take up the rest of her notice. By the time she was discharged her time in Bramble Bay would be officially over.

She would be able to go back to England and...what? Spend the rest of her life longing for Lafe Hilliard who had found her to be economical with the truth?

As the theatre doors swung open to let the trolley through, Suzannah had never felt so lonely. John and Debbie would have been there if they'd known. Or maybe Shirley would have dashed to be by her side, but the only person she really wanted with her was Lafe... and he wasn't there.

The anaesthetist was behind her, waiting to send her into oblivion, and as limbo took over Suzannah wasn't to know that a big, capable hand had taken her limp fingers in his and put them to his lips.

Striding up and down in the waiting area like a caged animal, Lafe thought wryly that there'd been countless times when he'd observed the anxious relatives of patients doing the same thing and had felt like telling them to calm down. But it only needed one to be on the other side of health care to understand the anguish of those who could only wait and hope.

Arriving too late to have any discussion with those who were to operate on Suzannah, Lafe had been aware that his appearance beside her in Theatre hadn't been welcome at such a moment, but he couldn't have cared less.

The need to let her see that he was there had blotted out all reason, but he'd been seconds too late and now all he could do was wait.

He'd persuaded the manager of the lumber camp at Bramble Bay to fly him to Port aux Basques, and though he had no real liking for the fellow he'd been humbly grateful that the guy had been willing to do him such a favour.

In the way that news travels fast, Michael Ericson had heard about the mountain rescue and Suzannah's part in it and, remembering her tactful efficiency when he'd gone to the surgery and how she'd danced with him at the motel, he hadn't minded agreeing to the frantic blond doctor's request.

'Lafe Hilliard?' a voice questioned from behind, as Lafe stood gazing morosely through the window.

He swung round to find the surgeon who'd operated on Suzannah smiling at him from the doorway. 'The lady is in Recovery. The operation went well. The blood has been drained away and the vein repaired. You can see her whenever you want…and although this isn't probably the right moment, might I just say that we're mighty grateful for the work that you're all putting in at the satellite clinic. It has greatly reduced our workload and I'm sure that the patients are equally appreciative of your efforts.'

Lafe nodded, only half listening. All he could think about was Suzannah. 'Thank you,' he murmured. 'Unfortunately, Dr Scott is leaving. She's working out her notice at the moment, and by the time she's discharged from here her commitment to us will be up.'

As the other man nodded understandingly Lafe wondered why he was babbling on like this. Maybe it was because by saying it out loud he could accept the fact of it with better grace.

'I'm delaying you,' the surgeon said with a smile. 'Dr

Scott is still unconscious, but I'm sure that she'll be delighted to find you beside her when she surfaces.'

Unfortunately, it didn't quite turn out like that. As Lafe sat looking down at the pale face which was only partly visible beneath a wad of dressings, a winter dawn brought to mind other matters that needed his attention.

The staff at the clinic would have heard about what had happened, but since the moment that he and Suzannah had gone back to their cabins to change their clothes for the climb up the mountain, he'd had no contact with them.

They would be anxious to know how she was and when he was likely to reappear. He could tell them one thing, but not the other. Suzannah had come through the operation safely and was on the way to recovery, but when he would be returning he didn't know.

At that precise moment all he wanted was to be with her, and when she regained consciousness and was well enough to talk he was going to tell her—

'There's a call for you, Dr Hilliard,' a young nurse informed him. 'You can take it in the office if you wish.'

It was Linda, and almost as if she'd read his mind she was asking how Suzannah was and when he was coming back.

'I'm staying until I'm sure that she's out of danger,' he told her. 'I'll give you a ring tomorrow. In the meantime, I'm expecting you all to carry on as normal.'

With that he wished her a brief goodbye and quickly made his way back to the recovery ward, but his step faltered as he drew near her bed.

Dismay was making his chest feel tight. Michael Ericson was in the seat that he'd just left, holding her hand and stroking her battered face, and Suzannah, who was now conscious, was smiling weakly up at him with her heart in her eyes.

So that was it, Lafe thought bleakly. No wonder the fellow had been so eager to offer his services when he'd heard about what had happened.

The country and western night at the hotel came back to his mind. Ericson had been all over Suzannah then and he'd seen him hanging around the clinic a lot more than he would have thought necessary from a health point of view.

It looked as if she had tired of his own coldness towards her and had opted for a warmer climate, and who could blame her for that? He didn't much care for the fellow but it wasn't for him to judge. *He'd* had his chance and had blown it.

They were too engrossed in each other to notice him go, just as they hadn't been aware of his presence in the first place, and as Lafe went out into the bleak winter morning the ice around his heart made the temperatures outside seem mild by comparison.

The nerve-stretching urgency that had made him so desperate to get to Suzannah had gone. There was a different kind of urgency in him now. He wanted to get away. To be gone from Port aux Basques.

He'd satisfied himself that she was through the operation safely and now the only thing to do was make himself scarce, remove himself from where his presence was surplus to requirements. And if there was one thing he was sure of, he wasn't going to accept a lift back from Michael Ericson—even if he had to damn well walk all the way.

It transpired that there was no call to do that. A young nurse was about to take some leave and was intending to visit her parents in Stephensville. When she heard that Lafe was in need of a lift in that direction, the offer was there, and in the early evening he arrived back at the clinic.

Everyone was anxious to know how Suzannah was. Even Linda found time to think about someone other than herself for a short time, and when Lafe had given them the details of what had happened up on the mountain and Suzannah's subsequent airlift to undergo surgery on the cranium, he went wearily to his cabin to phone her brother and his wife.

They were appalled at the news and John said immediately that he would go to her.

'That would be good,' Lafe told him flatly. 'She has someone with her at the moment but I don't know how long he'll be able to stay.'

There was silence at the other end of the line and then John said slowly, 'You mean she's in a relationship?'

'It would appear so.'

'I see.'

I wish I did, Lafe thought grimly. She'd already had a bad experience with the guy back in England and now she was all smiles for Ericson.

Suzannah had gone under the anaesthetic with tears clutching at her throat but she came out of it to joy. As the black mists began to lift and she looked around her muzzily, she saw the outline of a man beside her bed.

There was the fair pelt of his hair, the tanned neck rising from the open collar of a leather jacket, and as he stroked her cheek she peered up at him in bleary thankfulness. It wasn't until the figure beside the bed spoke that she knew her rejoicing to be a mistake.

'Hi, Doc,' a rougher voice than Lafe's said, and she shrank back against the pillows. 'How goes it?'

Suzannah didn't answer the question. She had one of her own.

'Where's Lafe?' she croaked.

'Your boss, you mean? I've no idea. Were you expecting him?'

He wasn't going to tell her that he'd flown him to the hospital in a state of great anxiety, because if the guy had been really worried he would have been there now, instead of leaving the way wide open.

Suzannah shook her head and immediately wished she hadn't. It felt sore and very tender.

She closed her eyes. 'No. I'm not expecting him,' she said weakly. 'I just wondered...'

Her voice trailed away and a nurse's crisp tones came from behind. 'I'm afraid you're going to have to leave, Mr Ericson. Dr Scott is only recently out of Theatre and needs to be left to recover.'

'Sure,' he said easily. 'No visitors, eh?'

'Correct,' she said smilingly as they went out into the corridor. 'Dr Hilliard has already left the building.'

Ericson eyed her in surprise. So he didn't want a lift back, then?

By the time John appeared early that evening, Suzannah had been transferred to a small side ward, and when she saw her brother framed in the doorway her heart lifted. At least somebody cared about her, she thought. John and Debbie would always be there for her...even if no one else was.

'How did you find out that I was here?' were her first words as he hugged her gently.

'Lafe rang from the clinic. He was concerned that you should have someone with you.'

Anyone but himself, she thought wretchedly. But having no wish to burden John with her misery, she dredged up a smile and said, 'That was thoughtful of him.'

Her brother eyed her thoughtfully. He wasn't going to tell Suzannah that Lafe had mentioned a man friend. For one thing, it wasn't the right moment.

Debbie had been amazed. 'I thought that Suzannah was in love with the delightful Lafe!' she'd exclaimed when he'd told her what the man in question had said.

'Seems that you were wrong,' he'd said, and had vowed

that he would let his sister tell him about the new man in her life in her own time.

'You must come to us when they discharge you,' he suggested, taking in Suzannah's general listlessness and the white face beneath the dressings.

Suzannah shook her head. 'No, John. I've come to a decision. When I get out of here I'm going back home. I've been hiding myself away long enough. If Malcolm Stennet will have me back at the hospital, and he's told me often enough that he will, I'm going back to Chester.

'Working in the clinic with Lafe and the others has shown me that I still want to be in a medical situation. I'd thought that I would never, ever want to go back to that sort of thing, but I know that it's in my blood. It's what I've always wanted to do and I'm not going to be beaten by a mistake that I would give everything I possess to have prevented.'

'Good for you,' he enthused, 'but what about the man in your life?'

Maybe this was the moment when Suzannah was going to put him in the picture about the new boyfriend, he thought, but it wasn't to be.

'What about him?' she said flatly. 'He knows where to find me.'

As he eyed her in some perplexity the same nurse as before made another timely intervention on her patient's behalf.

CHAPTER ELEVEN

WHEN Suzannah asked about the injured teenager she was told that he was poorly but stable, with head injuries and a broken arm and leg.

'His parents want to come to see you as soon as you feel up to it,' the nurse told her. 'They're so grateful for what you did and worried that you should have been injured during the course of it.'

'I was the only one small enough to get down there,' she said with a smile. 'Otherwise I wouldn't have got a look-in.'

By the time they appeared beside her bed in the late afternoon of the following day there was better news about the boy. His condition had improved and he was out of Intensive Care.

'He says he's going to come to see you as soon as they'll let him,' his mother said, 'so do, please, be sure to tell him how crazy he was to go up on the mountain in such weather.'

'I think that he might have worked that out for himself, don't you?' she said. 'But I'll give it a mention.'

They'd all been to see her from the clinic except Lafe. Shirley had been the most concerned and Suzannah knew that she would miss her friendship when she got back home.

Linda had bounced in one afternoon with her usual brash confidence, and the diffident Jones couple, who had come with her, had seemed to be even more reserved in such close proximity to the nurse.

'Lafe is away,' Linda informed her. 'He's taken a week's

leave to go to Nova Scotia for the wedding of the woman that he worked with on Ice Station Mercury.'

'And so who's in charge?' Suzannah asked to divert attention from her gloom.

'Some old guy is filling in. He was a GP before he retired.'

She nodded absently. How could Lafe ignore her like this? They'd been friendly enough before the trauma up on the mountain. In fact, she'd thought that things might be coming right between them, but obviously she'd been wrong. Since watching her being put in the helicopter on that dreadful day, he'd never been near her.

As if Alison guessed her thoughts, she said gently, 'He does enquire each day as to how you are, Suzannah. I'm sure that he's as anxious to have you back as we are.'

'I'm not coming back, Alison,' she said awkwardly. 'I've been working out my notice these last three weeks, and by the time I'm discharged it will be completed. I'm going straight back to England from here.'

'Does Lafe know?' they chorused.

'Yes, of course.'

'And he's not bothered?' Linda questioned, nonplussed for once.

'No, he's not bothered,' Suzannah assured her. 'Not bothered at all.'

John came for her on the day she was discharged, and he asked a couple of times if there was anyone she wanted to say goodbye to. He'd decided that if there was a man friend, he was keeping a very low profile.

'Only the staff,' she told him. 'I've already said my farewells to the folks at the clinic. They all rang up last night.'

'Lafe amongst them?'

He was watching her face, but it was completely blank.

'Er...no. Lafe is in Nova Scotia. He's gone to the wedding of a friend.'

'So he doesn't know that you're going back to England.'

'I haven't informed him personally but, no doubt, someone at the clinic will have told him.'

'I see.'

You don't, dear brother, she thought dolefully, but why depress John with her disastrous private life?

They were going to drive to Deerlake where she would board an internal flight to St Johns, and the long journey to London's Heathrow would commence.

From there it wasn't too far to Chester, the birthplace of the man whose medical skills and cool courage had been like a beacon, guiding her into a medical career. A career that she might have given up on if it hadn't been for a golden-haired Viking.

Don't think about him, she told herself firmly as the homeward flight took off. He was there for you once when you needed him. If he wasn't around the second time it was because he was disappointed in you...and you did give him cause.

All very logical reasoning, but it didn't make her feel any better.

Suzannah hadn't been back very long but she hoped that in the familiar surroundings that had been so much a part of her life before she'd gone to Newfoundland the terrible feeling of loss might disappear.

But the beautiful river reaches and winding streets with their quaint old buildings had done nothing to deaden the pain. Her love for her birthplace was a very different thing to the torrent of feeling that Lafe Hilliard had aroused in her.

Instead of seeing the ageless charm of the famous town, Suzannah saw wooden houses beside the blue Atlantic, with fishing boats moored nearby and the dense sparkling whiteness of snow upon snow. But most of all, in her mind's eye, she saw Lafe—tall, strong and so memorable that her heart almost stopped beating every time his face came to mind.

She was due to start back at the hospital. Malcolm had been as good as his word, reminding her that leaving the place had been of her own choice, and if the rest of her existence was a dead thing, the time she would spend on the wards was something to live for.

It was going home to her small rented flat that was the hard thing, and often she would sit staring into space in the evenings, reliving the time she'd spent with Lafe.

Christmas was very near and Suzannah could imagine the hustle and bustle in her brother's house, the excitement of the children and the heightening of the special togetherness that John and Debbie shared.

She wasn't envious. They worked at their marriage and loved each other deeply, so they deserved that there should be happiness in their home.

Both of them would have dearly liked her to have been part of their festivities, but if she'd stayed on in St Anthony there would have been the possibility of meeting Lafe. And if he'd ignored her presence then, as he had done while she'd been in hospital, it would have been more than she could have borne.

Suzannah had volunteered to work over the festive season. She had nothing planned and it would give staff with families the chance to spend more time with them. As for herself, she would have less time to wish for what might have been.

The wedding made Lafe feel even more out of sorts than he was already. Serena was a beautiful bride, but all the time he was observing her he was seeing another face above the elegant bridal gown and another body inside it. Which made him wonder if he would be going back to the news that Suzannah was going to be the next one to plight her troth.

He'd followed her post-operative progress zealously, checking each day with the hospital that she was having no recovery problems, and if the clinic staff had thought it strange that he'd made no attempt to visit her, he'd let them think it. He'd told himself that the last thing he wanted was to come face to face with the lovebirds.

That the wedding was at the same time as Suzannah's departure was a relief. He didn't have to stand by and watch her disappear out of his life.

He knew that she was going straight back to England. Shirley had packed all her stuff at the clinic and taken it to Port aux Basques so that there would be no need for her to return.

By the time he got back from the wedding she would be gone. Whether Ericson would be with her remained to be seen, but the first time he'd seen him since that night in the hospital the guy had looked like a cat with a saucer of cream.

It was on the day that he arrived back in Bramble Bay after the wedding that he found out why.

The day of Christmas Eve turned out to be a hotchpotch of happenings. The first was a heavy fall of snow during the previous night, which brought back painful memories. The second was the arrival of Father Christmas on the wards, and after that, for those well enough to enjoy it, the day became a round of festivities.

As Suzannah examined a fretful toddler, recovering from a terrifying bout of meningitis, a young nursing orderly came to tell her that Mr Stennet wanted to see her in his office as soon as she was free.

Her heart sank. What did Malcolm want her for? She'd imagined him to be long gone, with Christmas being so near, but she should have known better. The hospital was his life. His wife was dead, his children living abroad, so there was nothing for him to rush home for. That was something they had in common.

When she knocked on the door of his office and was invited to enter, it didn't dawn on her that the voice wasn't his. But when she went in and saw the outline of the man standing in pale winter sunlight by the window, she didn't make the same mistake again.

The breadth of him almost blotted out the sun, but there was enough of it getting through to highlight the golden thatch on his head and to pick out the strong planes of the face that was always before her, waking or sleeping.

'Hello, Suzannah,' Lafe said softly. 'Guess you're surprised to see me.'

'Yes, I am,' she croaked. 'You're the last person I was expecting to find in Malcolm's office. Where is he?'

'He's made a tactful departure.'

She was shaking with shock but her voice was cool enough as she commented, 'I would have thought you'd have wanted him to stay, as you've shown yourself to be so wary of my company.'

'That was because I'm an idiot,' he said with the quizzical smile that made her bones melt. 'I thought you had something going with Michael Ericson.'

Suzannah stared at him. 'What? I hardly know the man! Whatever gave you that idea?'

'He was seated beside you in the hospital, holding your hand and stroking your face...and you were looking up at him as if his presence was the only thing that mattered.'

'You were there?' she asked incredulously.

He nodded and said with a wry smile, 'Yes. I was. I'd browbeaten him into flying me to Port aux Basques, so desperate was I to get to you, but the moment my back was turned you and he appeared to be a couple, or so it seemed.'

'Oh, Lafe,' she breathed. 'I was still doped from the anaesthetic. I thought he was you. I could just make out the shape of him and his colouring, and I thought that all my miseries were coming to an end. But, instead, I never had you visit me once during my stay in hospital, which made me come to only one conclusion—that I was still unforgiven. So much so that you didn't even care whether I lived or died.'

'I cared all right. I was never off the phone, checking up on you, but apart from that I felt that if you'd transferred your affections to Ericson I must keep my distance.'

'Transferred!' she cried. 'There wasn't anything between Ericson and myself. My feelings for you had more substance than that!'

Lafe hadn't moved from his position by the window and neither had she shortened the distance between them, and the thought came to her that this was probably the most important conversation of their lives and they were conducting it like strangers.

'I know all that now,' Lafe said sombrely. 'When I got back from Serena's wedding and saw that he was still around, I tackled him about it and was told the same that you've just told me. That there was nothing between you. Apparently Ericson was just concerned about you, and in any case he's in a relationship. You'll never guess who with.'

'I've no idea.'

'Linda.'

She smiled. 'They might make a good match.'

'And what of us, Suzannah?' he asked softly. 'What sort of a match are we?'

'That's for you to say,' she said as her throat muscles

tightened. 'I know what I think, but it's what you have to say that counts. You've never forgiven me for not telling you about my dreadful mistake, have you?'

He was moving now, and in a couple of purposeful strides he was encircling her in his arms.

'Of course I have,' he murmured against her hair. 'We're only human, like the rest of the population, and you, my beautiful English doctor, were betrayed by someone who was supposed to care for you. I admit that I was put out when you first told me, but it was from the point of view of our relationship. I was so much in love with you I couldn't believe you would keep such a thing from me.'

Suzannah was trying to swallow but couldn't. 'You're using the past tense,' she said hoarsely. 'Don't you love me any more?'

His arms tightened. 'Of course I do! I've come all the way from Newfoundland in the hope of being forgiven for the way I wasn't there when you needed me.'

Her bones felt as if they would melt with joy and the tightness had gone from her throat as she told him gently, 'I've loved you from the moment you looked down on me from the wooden platform beside Wilfred Grenfell's memorial. You took my breath away then and you always will.'

Lafe was smiling now, the gravity gone. 'Do you remember the night we spent together?' he asked.

'Of course,' she said. 'I thought that I was going to have to live off that for the rest of my life.'

He shook his head. 'Not any more, my darling. We have countless nights and days ahead of us.'

'But how? Not with you in Canada and me here in England.'

'That isn't how it's going to be. How do you think I came to be here in the hospital?'

'I have no idea.'

'I came for an interview. Your very good friend Malcolm Stennet and other members of the trust have just spent a very amicable hour with me, and very soon I'll know if I'm to fill the vacancy for a general consultant.'

'What about the clinic at Bramble Bay?'

'My term was up. I could have stayed on, of course, but I did tell the authorities in the beginning that I wanted it to be a short stay. It was an experiment and I was chosen to get it off the ground.'

Her eyes were filled with memories of the ever-encircling sea, the lakes like blue glass and the frosted beauty of the icy wilderness.

'I'll never forget the time we spent there,' she said softly.

'Especially those moments down the hole in the mountain,' he reminded her quizzically.

She shuddered. 'Don't remind me. Instead, tell me how you knew where to find me.'

'Simple. John and Debbie told me...and they send lots of love and good wishes.'

'I can't believe that you persuaded the hospital hierarchy to interview you on Christmas Eve,' she said dreamily. 'They aren't usually around at this time.'

He laughed. 'I'm a very persuasive man... and I couldn't get here any earlier. I had to leave everything in order at the clinic.'

'You are indeed,' Suzannah agreed, joining in his laughter. 'And to think that I was resigned to spending Christmas alone.'

'You won't ever be alone again,' he told her with sudden seriousness. 'If I don't get the job here, there will be others not too far away.'

'You'll get it,' she promised tenderly. 'I can't resist you and neither will they, but I might have other plans.'

'Such as what?'

'Living in a beautiful old house by the sea in St Anthony

with my husband and children and my young nephews not far away.'

His face was alight.

'Is that really what you want?'

'Yes, Lafe,' she said softly. 'That's what I want.'

MILLS & BOON®
Makes any time special™

Mills & Boon publish 29 new titles every month. Select from...

Modern Romance™   Tender Romance™

Sensual Romance™

Medical Romance™   Historical Romance™

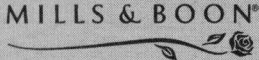

Medical Romance™

COMING HOME TO DANIEL by Josie Metcalfe
Denison Memorial Hospital

Believing that Daniel had died five years ago, Sam had comforted herself that at least she had his son to care for. But on returning home to take up a new locum position, she found Daniel alive and well—with a son only a few months older than their own!

DR MATHIESON'S DAUGHTER by Maggie Kingsley
Book two of St Stephen's Accident and Emergency duo

When Specialist Registrar and confirmed bachelor Dr Elliot Mathieson finds out he's a father, he begs his good friend, nurse Jane Halden for help. She can't refuse him, though maybe she should. Unknown to Elliot, Jane's been in love with him for years!

THE NURSE'S DILEMMA by Gill Sanderson
Book one of Nursing Sisters duo

Kate had always been a wanderer, but when she returned home, she found a reason to stay in Dr Steve Russell. However, he loved Kate because she wasn't looking for commitment and if she told him she loved him, she'd almost certainly lose him...

On sale 1st June 2001

Available at most branches of WH Smith, Tesco, Martins, Borders, Easons, Sainsbury, Woolworth and most good paperback bookshops

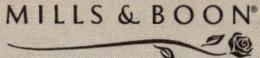

Medical Romance™

THE HONOURABLE DOCTOR by *Carol Wood*
Book one of *Country Partners* duo

Dr Marcus Granger and Dr Jane Court had been passionately in love, but she let Marcus marry her best friend, who was pregnant and terminally ill. Seven years later, widower Marcus is back. Can Jane ever forgive him for doing the honourable thing?

A HUSBAND TO TRUST by *Judy Campbell*

The day Mike Corrigan joined St Luke's as the new casualty doctor was the day that Sister Lindy Jenkins should have been married. Mike made it clear he was attracted to Lindy but if she risked her heart again, could he really be a husband to trust?

MIDWIFE UNDER FIRE! by *Fiona McArthur*

Midwife Noni Frost's maternity unit desperately needs to hire a new obstetrician, or it will be closed down. Obstetrician Iain McCloud tells her he is just a surgeon as he has reasons why he can't stay. But then he falls for Noni—how can he tell her the truth?

On sale 1st June 2001

Available at most branches of WH Smith, Tesco, Martins, Borders, Easons, Sainsbury, Woolworth and most good paperback bookshops

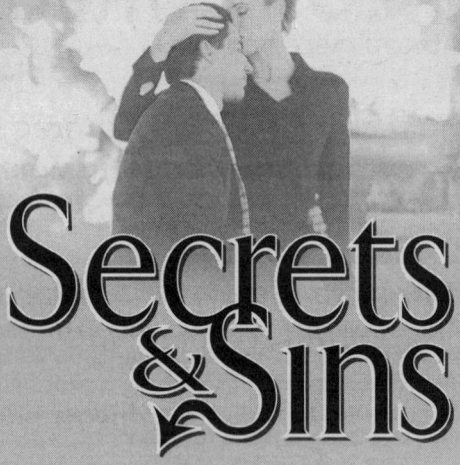

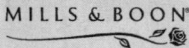

IN HOT PURSUIT

Nat, Mark and Michael are three sexy men, each in pursuit of the woman they intend to have...at all costs!

Three brand-new stories for a red-hot summer read!

**Vicki Lewis Thompson
Sherry Lewis
Roz Denny Fox**

Published 18th May

Available at branches of WH Smith, Tesco, Martins, RS McCall, Forbuoys, Borders, Easons, Sainsbury, Woolworth and most good paperback bookshops

FREE!
4 Books
and a surprise gift!

We would like to take this opportunity to thank you for reading this Mills & Boon® book by offering you the chance to take FOUR more specially selected titles from the Medical Romance™ series absolutely FREE! We're also making this offer to introduce you to the benefits of the Reader Service™—

- ★ FREE home delivery
- ★ FREE gifts and competitions
- ★ FREE monthly Newsletter
- ★ Books available before they're in the shops
- ★ Exclusive Reader Service discounts

Accepting these FREE books and gift places you under no obligation to buy; you may cancel at any time, even after receiving your free shipment. Simply complete your details below and return the entire page to the address below. *You don't even need a stamp!*

YES! Please send me 4 free Medical Romance books and a surprise gift. I understand that unless you hear from me, I will receive 6 superb new titles every month for just £2.49 each, postage and packing free. I am under no obligation to purchase any books and may cancel my subscription at any time. The free books and gift will be mine to keep in any case.

M1ZEB

Ms/Mrs/Miss/Mr .... Initials ....
BLOCK CAPITALS PLEASE

Surname ....

Address ....

....

.... Postcode ....

Send this whole page to:
UK: The Reader Service, FREEPOST CN81, Croydon, CR9 3WZ
EIRE: The Reader Service, PO Box 4546, Kilcock, County Kildare (stamp required)

Offer not valid to current Reader Service subscribers to this series. We reserve the right to refuse an application and applicants must be aged 18 years or over. Only one application per household. Terms and prices subject to change without notice. Offer expires 30th November 2001. As a result of this application, you may receive further offers from Harlequin Mills & Boon Limited and other carefully selected companies. If you would prefer not to share in this opportunity please write to The Data Manager at the address above.

Mills & Boon® is a registered trademark owned by Harlequin Mills & Boon Limited.
Medical Romance™ is being used as a trademark.